Heartlines

Books by Pam Lyons

A Boy Called Simon
He Was Bad
It Could Never Be
Latchkey Girl
Danny's Girl
Odd Girl Out
Ms Perfect

Books by Anita Eires

Tug Of Love
Summer Awakening
Spanish Exchange
Star Dreamer
Californian Summer
If Only . . .
Teacher's Pet
Working Girl

Books by Mary Hooper

Love Emma XXX
Follow That Dream
My Cousin Angie
Happy Ever After
Opposites Attract

Books by Barbara Jacobs

Two Times Two

Books by Jane Pitt

Loretta Rose
Autumn Always Comes

Stony Limits
Rainbows For Sale
Pia

Books by Ann de Gale

Island Encounter
Hands Off

Books by Anthea Cohen

Dangerous Love

Books by David S Williams

Give Me Back My Pride
Forgive and Forget

Books by Jill Young

Change Of Heart
Three Summers On

Books by Ann Ruffell

Friends For Keeps
Secret Passion
Baby Face

Books by Lorna Read

Images
The Name Is 'Zero'

Books by Jane Butterworth
Spotlight On Sam

Books by John Harvey
Wild Love

Heartlines

John Harvey

Wild Love

A Pan Original

First published 1986 by Pan Books Ltd,
Cavaye Place, London SW10 9PG
987654321
© John Harvey 1986
ISBN 0 330 29332 X

Printed and bound in Great Britain by
Hunt Barnard Printing, Aylesbury, Bucks

I thought I had left you behind
But find in others' eyes
The brightness of your own
The softness of your skin
On every stone

Chapter 1

Jane didn't think her father's car was going to make it. The hill rose from such an acute angle that they had to use a turning circle further along the main road and then approach it from the opposite direction. They climbed rapidly, so that from her passenger window Jane had what amounted to an aerial view of Hebden Bridge – the sun reflecting off the winding surface of its river and making the pale stone of its mills look special. She sensed her father changing down yet again as they were forced to slow almost to a halt behind a milk float that was crawling along in front of them. Jane glanced at her father, then at the position of the gear lever: she might not have passed her test yet, but she knew that the car was already in bottom gear. If the hill got any steeper – or the milk float got any slower – they would be in real difficulties. For a few seconds, Jane imagined them sliding back down towards the valley town more hastily than either of them wished.

But a right-hand fork appeared and the float wobbled its way in that direction, allowing the car to pick up a little speed before the road narrowed again and rose towards the small village ahead.

Her father leaned towards her and grinned with relief — an expression which changed smartly as a delivery lorry pulled out from a slip road and blocked their path. Richard grabbed at the hand brake as he jammed his foot to the floor. The car skidded first to the right, then the left, before coming to a halt with its rear wheels angled towards a low stone wall.

Unconcerned, the lorry was driving slowly out of sight around the corner and into the centre of the village itself.

'Are you all right?'

Jane nodded. 'Just about. But how's the car?'

He raised an eyebrow. 'We'll find out soon enough.'

The engine had cut out when Richard made his emergency stop, but it fired immediately and they slewed back on to the road and followed in the lorry's wake. Of course, it had come to a halt just round the corner and was preparing to unload outside a small grocery shop. The driver waved cheerily at their car as it swung out and tried to squeeze past them, a broad smile on his face which might or might not have been an acknowledgement of what he had done.

Richard raised a hand in greeting and immediately found himself turning left and facing yet another steep climb.

'You didn't tell me mountaineering experience was necessary,' said Jane, only half-joking.

Her father laughed. 'Why else d'you think we've got those oxygen containers in the boot?'

Jane had time to notice an attractive little square

over to the left, flanked on two sides by what appeared to be a pair of churches, one in ruins, the other seemingly in use. She would have to walk back down there and take a proper look when she had time – and her camera.

Richard changed gear as they went past school and post office and the road actually seemed to be levelling out. A thrust of power took them up on to the top and suddenly everything changed.

'There!'

The moors stretched out before them, folding away from either side of the ribbon of road until they became blurred in a distant horizon of sun-capped mist. Jane had an impression of an overall browny-green, interrupted here and there by solitary trees and patches of what she took to be heather – or was it gorse? The car continued slowly into this new landscape, her father peering through the windscreen as he drove.

'There's supposed to be a sign.'

'Saying Mill House?'

'Saying something.'

A couple of hundred yards further on, Jane shouted and pointed at the same time. Richard brought the car into the grass verge and looked.

'I can't see anything.'

'There. On the ground.'

She let herself out and hurried to where a signpost lay between the stone wall marking the beginnings of the moorland and the road. Turning it over, she read: *Mill House Arts Centre, next left ahead.* Straightening, she swung her head round and gazed out over 'the tops' – the moorland heights. The impression was of an immense space, pressing back against the sky; of loneliness and emptiness, but beauty too. A severe beauty.

And of something mysterious, somewhere out there in that desolate landscape.

Jane shivered and turned back towards the car. It must be colder than she had thought.

'Next left,' she said to her father, climbing back in.

'Whatever you say.'

But the next left proved to be little more than a track, pitted here and there with ruts that looked as if they would seize the car and shake the remaining life right out of it.

'It can't mean here.'

'That's what it said.'

'But this isn't a road.'

Jane shrugged her shoulders and sat back as the first serious doubts she had entertained since leaving Nottingham came into her mind. Had she really said she would spend a year up here? Trapped somewhere in this godforsaken countryside at the end of a road that was almost impassable. Even assuming they were able to crawl down there – what sign was there that they would ever be able to drive back up again?

'Hold on tight,' her father warned. 'Here we go!'

The car lurched forwards and hadn't gone more than ten yards before one of the rear wheels dipped into a pot hole and shook the wheel almost out of Richard's hands.

Father and daughter exchanged glances: without

needing words, they were both experiencing the same doubts.

The car inched forwards and down.

Every yard now jolted and banged so that it seemed the bottom of the car must fall out as they descended. The track turned right and then left and there below was the first glimpse of chimneys through a grove of dark green trees.

A smile ghosted across Richard's face and he depressed the accelerator as hard as he dared. Jane called a warning and he slowed down again, the wheels slurring dangerously close to the right bank.

'It would be a shame to break down now,' she said, gritting her teeth and keeping her arms braced against the dashboard.

'Absolutely!' agreed Richard and then smiled as the track widened and levelled out just ahead. The building was to their left now, its upper floor visible above a high stone wall. Below them the track continued on down to the bottom of the valley and from that point on it seemed to be impenetrable other than on foot. The car made a three-point turn and passed through an open five-bar gate and ran carefully down past the back of the house and came to a halt a little way beyond the door.

'Is this it?' Jane asked, looking doubtful.

'It has to be.'

'Well, it looked a lot different in the photograph.'

'I think that was taken from the far side of the valley, looking at the front of the house.'

Anything else Richard might have said was cut short

by the arrival of a black and white sheepdog that jumped up at the side of the car and proceeded to bark shrilly and show a nicely pointed set of teeth. The dog was followed hastily by a plump woman whose grey hair was tied in a plait around her head and who was rubbing her floury hands down the front of her apron as she walked.

'Prince! Come on away!'

The dog backed off as told, only to leap forward again as Jane and her father got out from the car. Jane gave the dog a quick glance and decided that discretion was far and away the better part of valour. She thrust her hands deep into her pockets so as not to give the animal anything to jump up at and set his teeth into, all the while doing her best to glare back at it in the unfrightened manner she'd been led to believe dogs understood best.

'No need to be frightened of him, miss. He's only pleased to see you.'

Jane tried to imagine what he would be like if he were angry – then she thought better of it.

'Mrs Hudson,' said Richard, going towards the woman and holding out his hand. 'I'm Richard Walker. And this is my daughter Jane.'

They all shook hands and exchanged words about the drive up from the Midlands. Seeing that they were welcome strangers, the dog rubbed against them, inviting hands to stroke and pat him. Mrs Hudson opened the tall arched door and ushered them inside. Within minutes they were sitting in a spacious room at the front of the house, a brick fireplace dividing it into two halves. Broad windows looked out on to a kitchen garden and then, beyond yet another stone wall, a field that dipped quite sharply down to the foot of the valley. At the far side, they could see a whitened track carving its way between scrub and small wiry fir trees.

Jane and her father sat on a long, comfortable settee facing the empty fireplace. Another settee was at right angles to theirs, placed underneath the window. Arm chairs, with loose covers in the same patterned material, were placed at either side of the fire. In winter, Jane could imagine roaring log fires and a busy atmosphere of conviviality and warmth. Now, with the light streaming in through the windows, the place seemed airy and free, almost liberating.

Mrs Hudson brought in a tray with a large brown teapot, cups and saucers and a plateful of home-made scones. She set it down on the long low marble-topped table and straightened herself with a small groan as something clicked in her back.

'Not as young as I used to be,' she smiled at Jane. 'But I thought you'd like some tea before you looked around. Not that I'm going to be looking after you like this every day, mind.' She folded her arms and seemed to be talking again to Jane rather than to her father. 'I come in most days and help straighten up a bit, do a little cleaning and make sure the place is generally to rights. But most of the real work, that's for you to do, miss. You won't find me one to interfere – not once you've found your bearings.' She moved towards the

13

door. 'I'll be in the kitchen, Mister Walker, if you want a word. I thought, seeing as it was your first night, you might fancy a little steak and kidney pie. Just to set you going, mind. I dare say your young lady there's a fine cook.'

Richard poured the tea and kept his tongue firmly in his cheek until Mrs Hudson had departed from earshot.

'Well, she seems to have got your work cut out for you.'

'Right. I'm slaving over a hot stove while you do all the exciting things.'

'Don't be hard on her, Jane. It's probably the only way she knows.'

Jane buttered two scones and passed one to her father. Taking it, he leaned back against the cushions and immediately she could see how tired he was after the drive. That and what this day meant for him – for both of them – a new job, a new place to live, a year spent together which after the divorce had not seemed possible.

She reached across and gently took the plate from his hand, setting it back on the tray. She heard the tone and tempo of his breathing change and knew that it would be some time before he woke. When he did, his energy would be restored and Jane knew she would see the same enthusiasm in him as on the evening, not so long before, when he had first told her about Mill House.

It had been in the Polish restaurant in Nottingham

and Richard had taken her there to apologize for missing her birthday party the night before. Or so she had thought . . .

Chapter 2

Jane had been looking her best. She had worn her favourite white dress with a loose red belt, white tights and soft red shoes. Twists of red glass hung from her ears. Her hair, dark and curled and almost shoulder-length had glistened as she turned her head towards the waitress. Until no more than a year ago she had been uncertain about her appearance; going out to dinner in a place where they had candles on the tables and kept the wine bottle in a silver ice bucket would have filled her with alarm. But that was before, that was when she was young, still a girl with ink stains on her fingers who didn't know what she wanted out of life. That had been before her A levels, before photography and boys had come into her life, before she had realized just exactly what she wanted to do with her life. Or thought she had . . .

Throughout the first course they chatted amiably about nothing in particular, skirting round the celebrations for her eighteenth birthday without touching on the reasons for his absence. Jane drank her wine slowly, ate her (delicious!) poached pastry pockets, wondering what her father was leading up to.

With the arrival of the main course she began to find out.

'Listen . . .'

'Umm.' Jane's mouth was too full to say more.

'You know how sorry I was about yesterday.'

Jane looked back across the table at him: did he know, she wondered, exactly how sorry she had been?

'Maybe when I explain . . . ' He glanced away from her for a moment, took a bite from the fish he had ordered for himself, and made a face that suggested it was as good as he had expected.

Jane cut into her beef, but no more. Why on earth couldn't he get on with it, instead of making such a big drama out of everything?

'I had this phone call in the afternoon. From an arts organization in London. I'd applied to them a couple of months ago for a job, two jobs actually. One was similar to what I was doing before. Publicity and so on. The other was administrative: running an arts centre in Cardiff. Bit of a wild shot, really, but it sounded interesting and I've got some experience.'

He broke off to look at her directly.

'You aren't eating,' he said.

'I'm listening.'

'Can't you do both?'

Jane sighed and tried some of the beef and then an

onion ring. 'Okay,' she said, 'now I'm doing both. Except that you've stopped talking.'

Her father grinned and drank some more wine, refilling his own glass and offering to top up hers, which she refused.

'Anyway, as I said, they phoned me up yesterday morning and asked if I could come down to London that day. All pretty secretive about it on the phone, but I figured they wouldn't be asking me to make the journey if there weren't something in it. So, rather than risk the car, I took the next train.

'The first thing the man said when I got to his office was that both the vacancies I had applied for had been filled. Wonderful, I thought! Have I come all this way just to be told I'm still unemployed?

'Then he took a photograph from a folder and showed it to me: it looked like a big old brick house in the country somewhere, somewhere pretty wild, a hillside on the edge of the moors or something like that. He asked me if I knew where it was and I guessed Yorkshire. He smiled and said right so far. Next was did I know what it was. Well, I didn't, of course.

'Mill Bank, he said. I wasn't any the wiser. He was obviously having the time of his life teasing me, but he could see that I wasn't far from getting annoyed. So he put down the picture, folded his arms and got down to brass tacks.'

He glanced at Jane as if to make sure she was paying attention.

' "That's Mill House", he said. "It's our north of

England creative arts and writing centre. How would you like a shot at running it?"'

'Dad! That's wonderful!' said Jane, leaning across the table towards him.

He laughed. 'You haven't heard the rest of it.'

'Go on.'

'Well, they had had someone else all lined up to take the job and for some reason he had pulled out. They want me to start in two weeks' time. A one-year contract, renewable for two years if it works out.'

'That's terrific!' Jane managed to lean far enough and avoid candles and wine bottle and give her father a happy kiss of congratulation. Any sense of lingering disappointment about his failure to come to her birthday party disappeared now that she knew the reason. It was a perfect job for him. Perfect! And she could see in his eyes how happy he was.

He gave her a little more wine and they lifted their glasses in a toast.

'To Mill House!' he smiled.

'To Mill House,' Jane echoed, thrilled for him after months of disappointment.

Her father set down his glass and took her hands between his. 'There's just one other thing,' he said carefully, looking straight into her eyes. And at that moment something in Jane's stomach began its familiar cold turning.

To Jane, when she went over that moment in her mind afterwards, that pause seemed to go on forever.

Around them the room seemed to be hushed, conversation ceased, movement was stilled. Her father's words came to her from a greater distance than the space between them and yet there was no doubting what he had to say. The conversation was one that she would replay and replay throughout the next two weeks.

'There's a snag.'

'Yes?'

'A condition.'

'Yes?'

'One I can't fulfil on my own.'

Jane continued to look back at him and wait; she was aware that her arms were suddenly covered with goose pimples.

'The job calls for two people.'

'Oh.'

'A man and a woman.'

'But surely . . . '

He shrugged. 'That's what they insist upon. Because of the residents, I suppose. It's got to be a man and a woman.'

I knew it, thought Jane, I just knew it. This is what he's been building up to. He's met somebody and he's going to take her with him, some new woman he's going to be living with up there in Yorkshire.

'I want you to come with me.'

She started. Her mind blurred. She couldn't have heard him right; she hadn't heard him right. He leaned towards her and tried his most winning smile.

'Come and work with me at the centre.'

'But I can't. You're not serious?'

'Of course.'

'Dad!'

'It's only for a year.'

Only!

Jane reached for her glass and her fingers fumbled against the stem; the next thing she knew the glass was rolling up against the side of her plate and white wine was spreading across the cloth. Jane looked round in agony, blood rising to her cheeks.

'Don't worry about it.' Her father used his napkin to mop up the worst of the spillage. Out of the corner of her eye Jane saw one of the waitresses begin to come towards them and then stop, gestured away by her father's hand.

He put down the napkin and reached for her hand, but she pulled it away.

'Jane, you'd love it!'

'I doubt that.'

'You could give it a try.'

'What on earth would I do?'

'Help me run the place. Write letters, answer the phone, greet the residents, take visiting artists out to lunch at the local pub, dig the garden, cook supper, get to know a whole range of people you've never had the chance to meet before.'

'Dad, I'm going to college.'

'It'll wait.'

'What d'you mean, wait?'

'I mean they'll hold your place open for you. Most places prefer students to have had a year out between school and their degree course. And if you were involved in an arts centre, they'd be even more pleased.'

'But I've got a place now. For October.'

'And I've got a job right now. Except that I can't take it if you won't come with me.'

'You can find somebody else.'

'In a fortnight?'

'Advertise.'

'And expect to find somebody I can work with in close company for a year? It's less than likely. Besides, it would be good for us to spend the time together.'

'Good for you, you mean. And convenient.'

As soon as the words had sprung from her mouth, Jane regretted them. Apart from what she had said, there had been a sharpness about the way she had spoken which she could see had hurt. Her father leaned uncomfortably back in his chair and looked down at the table. Two half-eaten meals sat there getting colder by the minute.

'I'm sorry, I didn't mean that.'

'No,' he shook his head. 'You're right. I mean, part of you is right. But I can't think of anyone I'd rather do this job with, anyone who'd do it better.' He paused. 'Jane, we could get to know each other again. As adults. Two people working side by side. It might be our last chance. After that you'll be at college and then starting a career and a life of your own.'

She didn't know what to say; she didn't know how to react: when the evening had begun she had thought she knew precisely what she wanted and where she was going in her life. It had all seemed so simple, so straightforward.

'Jane, all I'm asking is a year out of your life. Is that too much to ask?'

A year out of her life: she had not given him her answer there and then. She had talked about it with her mother, her friends, her tutor at school, the admissions officer at the college. In the end she had made up her own mind. She would come, but on her own conditions: her friends could come and stay from time to time; she would have weekends back in Nottingham when she was getting bored with all that countryside; there would be time for her to carry on with her photography. And she was going to work with him as an equal, not some cross between a serving-maid and a secretary.

Richard had been so pleased that he would have agreed to anything she had asked. She glanced across at him now, a smile playing round the corners of his mouth even as he slept. Silently, she got up and left the room, intent upon exploring the house.

Chapter 3

A quick examination showed that the living room was paralleled by a long narrow kitchen, both rooms leading towards a large dining room which was divided almost in two by the biggest wooden table Jane had ever seen. It would seat twenty people without any difficulty and probably squeeze in a few more besides. Above the dining room were two bedrooms and she wondered if they were intended for her father and herself. The remainder of the upper floor was made up of three dormitories, each fitted out with a number of bunk beds, and above that Jane discovered two small attic rooms, one with two beds and the other equipped with a table and some chairs. There were two bathrooms squeezed in between the dormitories and another alongside the bedrooms above the dining room.

The house was enormous!

Trying to think what it must be like when twenty or more people were staying there, Jane wandered out to the front of the house. Chickens pecked here and there among the patches of vegetables and beds of flowers, or wobbled across grey flagstones in the direction of two outbuildings in which they seemed to roost.

Mrs Hudson came out of one of these buildings, carrying a basket of fresh eggs. Seeing Jane, she came towards her, a smile at the corners of her eyes. 'Getting to know the place, then?'

'Yes, well, trying to get my bearings, at least.' She turned towards the house and pointed up towards the first floor. 'Those two bedrooms at that end – are they for my father and me?'

'Bless you, no. Hasn't he told you? You don't live in the house at all. Them as ran the centre used to, but there was so much hubbub from the visitors and suchlike, they never got any sleep.'

'Where do we stay then? Not back up in the village?'

Mrs Hudson shook her head and looked down the kitchen garden towards a brick archway. 'You take a walk along there, my pet, see what you can find. Something more to your taste than two old rooms, I'll be bound.'

Jane did as she was directed and passed through the archway and into a second garden, this one almost entirely given over to vegetables. On the low wall a large and fluffy black and white cat was stretched out, sunning itself. Jane wondered who had colour co-ordinated the household pets as she paused to push her finger tips through the warm fur of the animal's underside. It purred and wriggled its head contentedly. Jane gave the cat a final stroke and moved on. There was another archway at the end of the garden, this one set into a high wall backed by fruit trees.

On the other side she saw for the first time the place

where she was to live for that year at Mill House.

Hidden in the slopes of the hill that came down from the track, shielded even further by its surrounding trees, was the cottage. It looked small and cosy from the outside, so appealing that Jane ran forward and peered through the nearest of the downstairs windows. She glimpsed a heavy old armchair with a hand-embroidered cover at its back, a small round rosewood table holding a vase of freshly-cut flowers, a rug on which another cat – this one all ginger except for a white splodge over one ear – sat curled and sleeping.

When Jane tried the door it opened to her touch.

She was in a small but clean kitchen, equipped with sturdy pans and solid white china. Through the doorway were the stairs that led up to two bedrooms and a bathroom and Jane chose the smaller of the two for herself, its narrow bed resting close against a latticed window that gave her the best view yet of the valley.

Three tall chimneys pierced the thickness of trees that lined the valley bottom, towering high into the air. The trees climbed a little more than halfway up the sides, petering out into scrub and finally becoming moorland where the land began to level out and spread away in either direction.

Jane wondered how long it would take her to walk down into the valley and then along – and what she might find when she did so.

One more look around her room and she hurried back downstairs. A quick check of the living room – time just to stroke this cat too – and then she was outside and heading back in the direction of the main house. As she went through the first archway, a movement caught her eye away to the right, something that shifted at the edge of her vision near the corner of what seemed to be a barn up through the vegetable garden. Jane could not even be sure she had seen a movement at all. But as she walked slowly on, the thought came back to her that something had, indeed, been there.

Something: or someone.

She walked through the second archway and there was her father coming towards her, still rubbing the sleep from his eyes.

'You woke up then.'

'Just a nap.'

'Oh, yes! You know what that is, don't you?'

'No, what?'

'A sign of getting old.'

'Old? Me?'

'Yes.' Jane tugged playfully just behind his ear. 'Like these.'

'These what?'

Jane put finger and thumb tight together and pulled hard.

'Ow!' Her father jumped back, clutching the side of his head, surprise in his eyes.

'These grey hairs!' exclaimed Jane in triumph, holding one of them up for inspection.

'If you keep doing that,' said Richard, 'I shan't just be grey, I shall be bald.'

'I expect you will be soon anyway.'

'Yes. With worry.'

'With age, you mean!'

Richard took a mock swing at her head and Jane easily ducked beneath it and started to run back towards the house. There was still a great deal she had to explore.

Together they went into what Jane had rightly assumed had once been a high barn. Much work and money had now divided its interior into a number of specialized working spaces: in one there was a pottery wheel and a kiln; in another a variety of equipment for print making; while a third space housed their office, complete with typewriter, photocopier, answering machine and a pile of envelopes waiting to be opened and attended to. Richard shut the door on that quickly and took Jane up on to the second floor.

Most of this space was fitted out as a drama studio, with spotlights fitted to tracks that criss-crossed the ceiling and a number of interlocking wooden blocks against the far wall. It was enough to encourage Jane to mount one of them and give forth with the first half-dozen lines from the balcony scene in *Romeo and Juliet*.

'Don't call us . . . ' her father joked.

'I'll have you know our drama teacher practically went down on her knees to get me to audition for the school play.'

'I thought photography was more in your line.'

'So it is.'

'Then why don't you take a look behind one of those doors over there?'

Jane glanced at him a moment, puzzled, then moved along the studio floor. There were two doors in the wall at the far end; she hesitated before trying the one on the left.

'Looks like a dressing room to me,' she called back.

'Try the other one.'

Jane did so without any great anticipation. But when she saw what was on the other side of the door, she shrieked with delight. Richard came slowly forward and by the time he had got to the doorway, Jane was standing in the middle of what had turned out to be a perfectly equipped darkroom, a radiant smile lighting up her face.

'You do believe in keeping secrets, don't you?'

Her father grinned. 'I thought it would be a nice surprise.'

'Nice! You're full of surprises. First the cottage and then this.' She gave him a hug of thanks. 'Why on earth didn't you tell me? Before, I mean. Then I would have jumped at the chance of coming.'

'I didn't want that to be the reason you said yes.'

Jane shook her head and smiled.

'It wouldn't have been, silly!'

'I know.' He laughed. 'I'm glad.' For a moment he held her hand. 'You know, we're going to have a great time.'

Jane held on to his arm as they walked back through

the drama studio. 'Yes, better than I'd ever dreamed it would be.'

He kissed her on top of the head and then stood to one side to let her down the stairs first. Together they walked back across the stone pavings to the house, each thinking that one more pot of tea before they began to tackle that pile of post wouldn't be too much to ask.

For just a moment before going inside, Jane turned back towards the barn and stared at the space between its wall and the garden beyond: wondering what or whom she could have seen.

Chapter 4

Jane was almost immediately deluged in a flood of activity, which gave her no time for thinking about mysteries of any kind – the only mystery was how she and her father kept from going under for the third and final time.

A quick look at the office calendar showed them that two courses were due to start in less than a week's time and that from that point on the centre was fully booked until the short Christmas break.

Jane breathed deeply as she saw her plans for weekend trips back to Nottingham cast aside; she sighed as she realized that it would not be possible for her to devote as much time to her photography as she had planned, until she had found a way of keeping her head above water. It was one thing to have written down a neat list of conditions of service and to have had it signed, but quite another to try and live up to them when faced with the enormous task of getting the centre running smoothly.

While her father took it upon himself to get in touch with the various writers and artists who were due to spend time at the centre, teaching and working, Jane began the arduous job of contacting those people who had written asking to be included on the various courses. So that, while Richard was talking on one telephone to a mime artist from Darlington – who wanted to make sure there would be sufficient plaster of Paris for making masks and a good supply of fluorescent paint for making them up – Jane was using the phone at the other end of the office to convince two spinster sisters from Mablethorpe that a short course on the poetry of the moors might be more suitable for them than a week participating in an introduction to African drumming and ritual dance.

'Yes,' Richard concluded, 'if you bring your own strobe light we can mix it through our lighting box.'

'Yes,' said Jane with as much conviction as she could muster, 'we can make sure that you have vegetarian meals during your stay.'

Simultaneously they put down the receivers: simultaneously they looked at each other and laughed. It was the only thing to do – other than bow their heads and cry.

There were:
— duvets and sheets to be retrieved from the laundry and fitted to the beds;
— basic supplies for the kitchen to be fetched from the Cash and Carry in the nearest town;
— clay for the pottery to be collected and unloaded in the workshop;
— typewriter ribbons and endless sheets of blank paper, erasers, ink, scribbling pads, pencils to be dispersed around the house for the writing groups;
— fresh supplies of walking maps of the area to be collected from the tourist office down in Hebden Bridge;
— rooms to be cleaned;
— chickens to be fed;
— more letters to be answered;
— more forms to be signed.
There was:
— more work to be squeezed in than there was ever going to be time for.

Jane and her father woke early and stumbled to the bathroom, fed the cats and other animals they had inherited and then fed themselves; too many hours later they stumbled back to their beds and fell asleep almost before their heads had touched their respective pillows.

All of this proved her father to have been right in one thing: it was impossible to imagine that he could have done all this with anyone else. They worked together without argument and when one of them made a mistake (as in those first few days often happened) the other picked up the pieces and carried on without a word of reproach. Jane felt more tired than she could remember, but she finished each day with a sense of satisfaction at what she had been able to achieve.

And when, at seven minutes past three on a sunny Saturday afternoon (it was a time both of them would remember for a long time) the door opened and the first of many faces peered round it uncertainly and said: 'Is this Mill House Arts Centre?' they hugged each other – and their astonished first visitor – with rib-threatening enthusiasm.

By the end of the first two weeks it was difficult to recall what all the fuss had been about. Everything seemed to be running as smoothly as silk. A drama group was finishing a week's work in the studio. The resident potter had started a series of pieces based upon the local area. A writer of short stories was persuading the most unlikely bunch of authors to produce even less likely stories of their own. Next week they were to play host to a folk singer from Scotland, a puppeteer from Norfolk and a young poet from no one was quite sure where.

Jane sat with her feet up on the office desk, drinking her umpteenth cup of coffee. The door opened quietly behind her and before she could turn her head or speak, a pair of hands fastened over her eyes.

'Guess who?'

'Michael Jackson.'

'Close.'

Richard sat on the edge of the desk and told Jane to close her eyes.

'I just did.'

'Do it again.'

From the sparkle in her father's blue eyes, Jane knew that he was up to something. She shut her eyes and waited.

'Now hold out your hands.'

'Oh, no.'

'Come on, do it. Hold out your hands. Not that far apart. No, that's too close together. That's it. Now keep them there, just as they are.'

Jane heard him reach inside his coat, then the sound of a paper bag being opened.

'If it's anything nasty . . .'

Richard laughed. 'Would I do something like that?'

'Yes.'

He laughed again and set it in her hands.

It.

Jane closed her fingers around it gingerly; nothing to worry about. 'It's a book,' she tried not to sound disappointed.

'Don't sound so disappointed.'

She hadn't succeeded.

'Aren't you going to see what it is?'

Jane slowly opened her eyes. Whatever it was, it was beautiful. The book was small with shiny marbled covers in purple and dark blue, the edges of the paper were silver and the inside covers were faded gold.

'It's lovely,' she said. 'Where did you get it?'

'I saw it in that second-hand bookshop down the hill days ago and sneaked back and bought it. I thought you deserved something special for all the work you've done.'

'No more than you.'

'I've already got my present.'

She looked at him questioningly. 'What's that?'

'You. Your being here.'

Jane smiled at him quickly and then looked away. Her fingers smoothed over the surface of her book then traced the letters of the title as they were cut into the spine: *Wuthering Heights*.

'She lived near here, you know.'

'I think I knew it was Yorkshire somewhere.'

'Haworth. It's just a little way over the moor. And the places she writes about in there. The heights. All you have to do is climb the hill and you're there. More or less.'

Jane kissed him on the cheek.

'You'll have more time to yourself now. You'll be able to get some reading done.'

'Don't forget my photography.'

'And some of your precious photography,' Richard laughed.

He headed for the door. 'Someone was asking for

some stamps. I'd better go and find them.' At the doorway he turned. 'You don't regret it, do you? Coming here, I mean. Instead of going off to college.'

Jane shook her head slowly and smiled. 'No, I don't regret it.'

'Good.'

Her father closed the door slowly and she heard him walk away. She swung back in her chair and opened the book at random . . .

Ellen, how long will it be before I can walk to the top of those hills? I wonder what lies on the other side . . .

Jane stood up and walked to the window; the day was bright, no more than a scattering of small clouds tarnishing an unbroken blue. She felt an urge to be outside, out there, striding up towards the moors with the sun on her back and the fresh air in her face and lungs. It took her less than ten minutes to get her boots and an anorak from the cottage and to shout a message to her father, telling him she would be back in plenty of time for tea. Then she was through the gate and the valley was ahead of her: she knew that the track would take her down to the first of the chimneys and from there a path should lead her along the river bank and finally up to the moor.

A bar of chocolate in one pocket and her book in the other, she set out.

Chapter 5

After she had been walking for little more than half an hour, the path Jane had been following came to a halt. There was a clearing in front of her and the dried earth showed no footprints leading off in any direction. Ahead, through the leaves of the trees, she could see the scarred brickwork of the second mill chimney; to either side, bushes and yet more trees seemed to be defying her to make her way between them. Jane searched the far side of the clearing for evidence of a new path but found none. Still, it was unlikely that she would get lost so close to home – and there were always the chimney-stacks to guide her.

Shortly, her faith was justified and she quickened her step as she found that she was on a path again, not as well-defined as the one she had followed first, but a path nevertheless.

Bracken closed in upon her gradually as she walked and here and there thorns and prickly branches clung to her jeans. For one moment that stopped her breath she lost sight of the chimney altogether and the beginnings of panic hit home. But almost at once, she found her bearings again, as the path turned and twisted back upon itself and before she knew it she was staring at the chimney's broad base.

Jane had not thought that the actual chimney would be so wide; when she stood close it blocked out the sun and she shivered involuntarily, as if — as her grandmother was fond of saying — someone had walked over her grave.

She moved to the other side of the chimney and positioned herself so that the sun could reach her through a gap in the trees. She sat down and leant back against the chimney and brought her book from her pocket. If she rested for ten minutes or so and did a little reading, that would leave her plenty of time to go on up the valley and still make her way back along the edge of the moor as she had planned.

Immediately Jane was caught up in Emily Brontë's world. She could see her hero Heathcliff clearly; his dark hair and his black eyes that blazed with an anger that was frightening and strangely attractive at the same time. She hugged her knees close as Heathcliff's dogs — *half-a-dozen four-footed fiends* — attacked a visitor without provocation. And turning her head to gaze through the bracken towards the desolation of the moor, she could feel herself at one with *On that bleak hill-top the earth was hard with a black frost, and the air made me shiver through every limb.*

She did shiver.

A shadow slid across the page and she shivered again.

Jane came slowly to her feet, one hand pressed back

against the hardness of stone. The sun had been covered from sight, blocked out by a cloud darker and blacker than any she had noticed in the sky when she had begun reading.

She glanced once more at the book and then shut it from her sight. As she did so something moved on the hillside before her. Something cracked thinly, a small sound that was swallowed by the surrounding silence before Jane could place its source.

Below her sight, the river rocked over its rocky bed.

A crow flew from tree to tree, unsettling the air.

There was somebody, in the trees, watching her.

Jane's eyes closed and the backs of her legs were like ice. The rough chimney-stone pressed hard against her back. She stood there waiting for something to happen: seconds that clung like minutes, like a black veil of frost drawn across the sun.

She made herself open her eyes.

The trunks of the trees surrounded her blankly. She turned her head cautiously, right and then left. Nothing moved. The last fragment of dark cloud fell away and the small clearing was washed with light.

Jane drew in air and stepped away.

Whatever had been up there, hidden from sight, watching her, had gone. Without seeing its departure, she could sense that now she was alone where just moments before she had been in the presence of another person.

The image of Heathcliff – surly, handsome and silent – rose up in her mind and Jane laughed aloud. She had been reading too many books. A girl of her age! She should know better.

She pushed the novel down into her pocket and cupped both hands to her mouth.

'Hello! Is anybody out there? Is there anyone there?'

She listened as the faint echoes of her voice shimmered between the trees, drifting back towards silence. Jane broke off a piece of chocolate and put it in her mouth; that left one more piece for when she got to the top and another for when she was halfway along the return journey. And none for stupid old Heathcliff!

She was well along the path before it came to her that no matter how powerful the writing was, no matter how vivid her own imagination – neither of them would have had the strength to break a stick at fifty yards.

Her father was in the kitchen when she returned to the yard; she saw him through the window, pouring boiling water into the teapot. Now that was what she called good timing!

'You're not coming in here in those muddy boots, are you?'

'Mud? I'd have had to have walked a lot further than I did to find mud. It's nothing but baked earth out there. Even right down by the river.'

'Mmm.' Richard poured milk into the cups, gave the teapot a quizzical look, decided it had brewed by now, and finished his task. 'I think that might change. And not before long.'

'There's hardly a cloud in the sky.'

'More than yesterday.'

'Even so.'

They sat on high stools in the narrow kitchen, Jane making sure that she was close enough to the farmhouse loaf that was waiting temptingly on the bread board. After a good walk there was little better than a real doorstep, liberally covered in raspberry jam.

'The important person here is Mrs Hudson's widowed sister. When she gets twinges in her right leg and her shoulders start acting up, that's a sure sign that the weather's going to break.'

'Mum's mother's always saying things like that and she's no better a weather forecaster than a bit of seaweed.'

'Maybe, but then she hasn't spent all her life in the country — close to nature.' He sipped his tea and gave it a look of satisfaction. Now if only Jane would get a move on with the jam . . . 'So next time you go for a walk, watch out. Take an anorak at least.'

'I did.'

'Oh.' A pause. 'Well, you always were a careful child.'

'I'm not a child any more.'

'But you're still careful. I hope.'

'What's that supposed to mean?'

'Nothing.'

'Then why . . . ?'

Richard got up and took the jam. 'It was just something that came out, that was all. I didn't mean anything by it at all. Besides, it would be a bit late in the day for me to start offering you that kind of advice, wouldn't it? I mean, you've managed pretty well up to now. I can't think of anyone I know whose daughter negotiated adolescence with so little difficulty.'

He smiled at her in what she supposed was meant to be congratulations, but it was a smile Jane didn't return. If you'd been around more of the time, she was thinking, you might have seen that growing up wasn't as painless as you're making out. That was when you should have been there, drinking tea and eating bread and jam with me while you offered friendly advice.

'Penny for them,' said Richard briskly, getting up to pour some more tea.

Jane shook her head, both to his question and the offer of another drink. 'They're worth more than that.'

'You're not off already?'

'I want to get out of these boots. My feet are starting to seize up. And then I'm going to do some more reading before suppertime. Okay?'

Richard waved a hand in agreement; before she had left the room the bread knife was back in his hand. There is no such thing, he was thinking, as *one* slice of bread and jam.

Jane had found the perfect place to read undisturbed. The landing on the stairs at the western end of the house was set against a broad arched window and there was a ledge there wide enough for her to sit on.

She leaned her back against one wall and, with her legs raised, rested her feet against the other. There was plenty of light from the window and because of the slope of the yard she did not seem to be perched very high from the ground.

From one room below came the inconsistent chatter of typewriters being used by a number of two-finger typists. Out across the yard, she could see two of the visitors in earnest conversation with the black-and-white cat. Chickens scuttled and pecked as the white cockerel strutted amongst them.

Jane read.

The visitor to Wuthering Heights, the isolated and windswept house on the moors where the violent Heathcliff was master, had been allowed to stay the night because of the storm that was raging outside. He was shown to a cold bedroom where he found a diary belonging to a young woman named Cathy – and as the visitor began to read the diary, the cold seeped deeper and deeper into his limbs and the wind howled all the more fiercely outside.

Jane could not lift her eyes from the page.

Wind and snow gusted against the window; the branch of a fir tree rattled against the pane. A hand pushed hard against the glass to open it, slipped and broke through; fingers reached for the branch to pull it aside, *instead of which, my fingers closed on the fingers of a little ice-cold hand!*

Jane's body jumped: the hand holding down the

white pages of the book was cold, as if laid against snow.

She wanted to put the book down but could not.

Her fingers seemed held fast to the page.

As the wind gathered it carried a voice within it, a sound that chilled more than any cold.

I pulled its wrist on to the broken pane, and rubbed it to and fro till the blood ran down and soaked the bedclothes . . .

Something tapped at the window: sharp and loud.

Jane's blood froze.

I tried to jump up, but could not stir a limb: and so yelled aloud, in a frenzy of fright.

The tapping continued through the sound of her voice. Jane had to force herself to turn her head towards the pane. What she saw made her scream again. A face was hard against the window: the face of a young man, swarthy and handsome, surrounded by dark and unkempt curly hair.

The book fell from Jane's fingers as she clasped her hands to her face, covering her eyes. When she moved them aside, no more than seconds later, the window was bare. There was no one in sight.

Chapter 6

'You look,' Richard said, 'as though you've seen a ghost.'

Jane sat in the cottage armchair and immediately the ginger cat jumped on to her lap and began to work its claws against her jumper. 'I have,' she said.

Her father studied her, half-amused. 'Oh, really. Whose ghost, exactly?'

'Heathcliff's.'

'Heathcliff! You *have* been taking your Emily Brontë seriously.'

'Except that it wasn't Heathcliff.'

'No, I didn't think it was. Not really.'

'Not exactly.'

He could tell from her expression, from her manner that what he might be likely to dismiss as a joke was far more than that for Jane.

'It is a very powerful novel,' he began, sitting on the edge of her chair and stroking the cat between its ears. 'I remember when I first read it . . . '

'It's not just the book.' Jane looked up at him. 'I mean, it is partly that. Of course it is. But somehow there's more.'

'You don't think it's being around all these writers and artists? A surplus of imagination rubbing off on you?'

Jane lifted the cat from her lap and moved towards the fireplace, turning to face her father when she got there. 'Whoever I saw at that window was no figment of the imagination. Mine or anybody else's.'

'And it wasn't one of the visitors?'

She shook her head.

'You're sure?'

'Certain.'

Richard thrust his hands down into his trouser pockets and shrugged. 'Then I don't know. Unless it was someone who just wandered in off the track. That's possible.'

Jane considered it; the way the person she'd seen looked in that moment he could have been walking on the moors and come down in search of – what? Something to drink or eat? Directions? Perhaps it had been natural curiosity? But none of those suggestions fitted in with the urgency Jane associated with the knocking at the window, nor the expression she remembered from his face. A strange mixture of strength and mystery . . . she laughed to herself. Heathcliff again.

'We'll have to keep our eyes open,' Richard said. 'Don't want strangers wandering all over the place without knowing who they are. There's a lot of expensive equipment around one way or another.' He clicked his fingers sharply. 'Which reminds me – did you ever sort out that premium with the insurance company?'

'Fire and theft, you mean?'

'That's the one. There was some argument about increasing the amount we were paying. I don't know if it was ever settled.'

'Nor do I.'

'But if I'm right, you were going to . . .'

'Yes, I was. And I'll get on to it now.' Jane vaulted past the armchair, startling both the cat and her father. She ran down the path and across the yard, bounded into the office and began shuffling through a pile of letters that had been pushed into a filing tray marked 'Pending'. If the insurance had lapsed and something had been stolen then it would be her responsibility: and she couldn't see her father's employers being very impressed with his efficiency. They certainly weren't going to be waving another two-year contract at him, that was a fact.

She pulled the letter clear, scanned it and reached for the telephone.

The evening had been a long one. After supper they had had a visit from a writer of stories about the supernatural. Listening to the woman read, in a surprisingly deep voice, as the light outside had waned, all of those present had responded with a chill of tingling fear. But no matter how skilful the writer was, she had not succeeded in getting to Jane as Emily Brontë had; she had not invaded the marrow of her bones.

Jane's sleep had been more troubled than usual, as if dreams were nagging at the windows of the mind, trying to force their way through. But finally sheer tiredness won out and Jane had fallen into a deep sleep in the hour before waking. So it was that when she left the cottage, bleary-eyed and far from 'together', she did not immediately take in the full meaning of what she saw at the end of the garden.

But there was Mrs Hudson deep in conversation with a tall, dark-haired young man, so like the sudden apparition at her window the previous afternoon that it could be no coincidence.

As Jane approached, the youth turned his head and, seeing her, walked swiftly away, slipping from sight round the side of the nearest outbuilding.

'Morning, miss,' greeted Mrs Hudson, her egg basket over one arm.

'Who was that?' Jane asked, looking in the direction the youth had taken.

'That, miss?'

'Yes. The person you were talking to. As I was coming up to the house. He hurried away as soon as he saw me.'

'I'm sure no one'd run from you, miss.'

'Who was it?' Jane's voice was raised to the point where Mrs Hudson looked back at her with some alarm.

'Oh, well, miss. I suppose you're talking about Gareth.'

'Gareth?'

'Yes, miss. That's who it must've been.'

And Mrs Hudson turned her back and headed into the chickens' roost to make her morning collection of eggs. Jane ran around her and blocked her path.

'You still haven't told me.'

'What, miss?'

Jane held on to her temper as fast as she could, but it wasn't easy. 'I would like to know exactly what or who this Gareth is.'

'Oh, that's simple, miss. He's from the village. Comes up here times to help out in the garden. Spring and summer especially.'

'You mean he works here?'

'Isn't that what I've been saying, bless you?'

'Works for us, Dad and me?'

'In a manner of speaking, yes, I suppose he does.'

'Then why on earth have we never seen him before?'

'I can't say for sure, miss. Though his old father has been sick these past weeks. I expect Gareth's been tending to him. Too busy to get up here, I shouldn't be surprised.'

'Then he works when he feels like it?' Jane couldn't keep the annoyance out of her voice.

'Oh, he's a good worker, miss. There's never been no complaints about Gareth's work. I can assure you of that.'

Jane looked around: once again there was no sign of him. 'If he's paid to do the garden, where is he? Not in the garden, that's for certain.'

Mrs Hudson sniffed. 'I can't say, miss. But there's all kinds of jobs want doing around the house. When you've been here longer, you'll come to understand. Meanwhile, miss, if you'll excuse me, I must be getting on.'

And she bustled past Jane, doing her best to look both hurried and efficient at the same time.

The sound of the car engine took Jane through the rear of the house, past the kitchen and out again into the yard. Her father was just pulling away as she ran towards him.

'Want something in town?' he asked, rolling down the window.

'You mean the village?'

He shook his head. 'I've got to go into Halifax. I thought I'd said.'

'I expect so. I'd forgotten.'

'And there's nothing you want?'

Jane stepped away from the car. 'No, thanks.'

'Okay.' Richard let the car into gear.

'What time will you be back?'

'Oh, early this afternoon. Somewhere around there. Does it make any difference?'

'No. I can manage.'

'Of course you can.' He winked at her, rolled the window back up and pulled away.

Jane stood where she was until the sound of the car was little more than a faint hum across the quiet of the morning. With a small shrug she turned round, and when she did so Gareth was standing in the arched doorway, staring straight at her.

Chapter 7

He was leaning against one side of the doorway, one arm angled across his body. Jane noticed the dark curls of his hair, the glistening dark of his eyes. His nose was arched a little at the bridge and his mouth was wide and full. He was wearing a pair of faded jeans pushed down into scuffed leather boots, a blue and green check shirt beneath the waistcoat from someone's old pinstripe suit. A dark green scarf was knotted loosely at his neck.

Jane was held by his eyes.

The surface of her skin was on fire.

'You're Gareth,' she said, almost as if wanting to prove that he was real.

'Who're you?' His voice was that of a man and no longer a boy. There was a hint of sullenness to it, a suggestion of contempt that was being held at bay — just.

'Jane. My father . . . '

'He's the new boss here.'

'I suppose so. Although boss doesn't sound right.'

'Not to you.'

Jane looked at him for an explanation.

'You're his daughter. He doesn't tell you what to do.'

'I wouldn't bet on it. And, besides, when was the last time he gave you orders?'

'Not directly p'raps.'

'I don't think he even knows you work here. Neither of us knew you worked here. Not until this morning when Mrs Hudson . . . '

'She talks too much.'

'If we don't know you're here, how on earth do you expect to be paid?'

She thought the beginnings of a smile showed behind the gleam of his eyes, but she didn't know him well enough to be sure.

'I shall be all right now, then. Now that you know me.'

Jane started to say something about the fact that she was by no means certain they could afford his help, however infrequent, when he cut across her words.

'I always had a good arrangement with them as were here before. I can't see no reason why it should be any different now.' He looked past her. 'Unless you and your father was thinking of taking on the gardens yourselves.'

'I don't think so. I don't think we'd have the time.'

'That's all right then.' He turned back into the house. The sound of music, something classical, came from the area of the drama studio. Jane watched him go, looked at the way the ends of his hair curled up against the back of his shirt and turned against his neck; she wanted to say something more to keep him there, but no words would come to her mind.

She was still standing there several minutes later when a middle-aged woman in a tweed suit, who was apparently the star of the present writing group, came over and coughed discreetly in her ear. Jane jumped and flushed red.

'I was just wondering,' said the woman, pretending not to notice Jane's embarrassment, 'if you could tell me when Martin McCabe is arriving?'

Jane's mind raced: Martin McCabe, Martin McCabe, Martin McCabe . . .

'He is due to join the course today, isn't he?'

'Er, well, I could check . . . '

'Your father said the seventeenth, I'm certain.' She tried a quick smile, tight-lipped but well-intentioned. 'We were all so excited that his time here would begin before our course was over. He's such a talented poet, don't you agree?'

'Yes, really good.' Jane moved away in the direction of the office. 'I'll go and check what time he is arriving. If you'd like to come with me . . . '

'Oh, no, just as long as it is today. We were hoping to persuade him to do a reading for us after supper. You don't suppose he'd mind, do you?'

'I really can't say,' called Jane as she hurried away. 'You'll have to ask him when he get here.'

The letter was close to the top of the action file, a note in her father's writing across the bottom. Martin

McCabe's train from London arrived at Hebden Bridge at two-thirty that afternoon and would be met: Jane supposed that meant her father was going to pick him up on his way back from Halifax. She sat behind the typewriter for a while trying to imagine what a poet from Edinburgh with a name like Martin McCabe would look like. She had a mixed-up picture of a man in his late fifties with a shock of grey, almost white, hair – smoking a Sherlock Holmes pipe and wearing a tartan waistcoat under his rough tweed jacket. No wonder the woman who'd spoken to her outside was so anxious to see him; they wouldn't only have a love of poetry in common, they would be able to swop stories about Highland tartans as well. She saw them sitting on one of the comfortable sofas in the house, the light fading as they talked on and on, boring everybody to death.

Outside the barn, in the space between two small fruit trees, three members of the drama course were staring intently into space, concentrating like mad, while their arms and fingers wound towards and away from one another like so many snakes.

Marilyn came out of the pottery studio and blinked at Jane through small round-framed glasses; the skin of her arms was red with clay or glaze or a combination of the two. She asked Jane if she had remembered a promise to come into the studio and photograph a batch of pots before the end of the week. Jane had. What she had to do now was check in the kitchen that all of the ingredients for the night's communal meal were at hand.

She was inside the kitchen looking out when she saw Gareth go past the window with a spade resting on his shoulder. So it was all the more surprising when the kitchen door was pushed open less than ten minutes later and Gareth came into the long narrow room. In order to get past Jane and reach the sink, he had to move very close to her. So close that if she happened accidentally to turn at the wrong (the right) moment . . .

'Oh, sorry!'

'That's all right.'

They stood looking at each other, their faces so close each could feel the faint warmth of the other's breath. She could see that Gareth's eyes were not simply dark: close to their centre green and brown swirled and chased and never seemed to be still. Yet his eyes were fixed upon hers.

'I didn't mean . . . '

Jane's words faltered to nothing. A slight curling of his lip told her that he knew only too well she was lying.

His bare arm was still inches away from her own.

His leg was so close to her's that she imagined she could feel the smoothness of the faded denim through the material of her cords.

'I just came in for a cup of tea.'

Jane didn't dare to move: if she did, there was no way of knowing what might happen. She felt as if she were balancing on a slack wire that she couldn't even see.

'I usually do . . . when I'm through work.'

'You've finished then?'

'For today.'

If he didn't move away soon, Jane thought she would burst — she would scream — she didn't know what she might do but whatever it was she wasn't going to be responsible for the consequences.

The sullen look about Gareth's mouth changed for no more than a second or two to that suspicion of a smile Jane thought she had noticed in the doorway earlier. Then he was holding the kettle beneath the tap and the water was splashing down into it and whatever the tension had been between them seemed to have evaporated.

For the present.

'Will you have a cup?'

'Yes,' Jane almost stumbled over the word in her haste to accept. Now, she thought, they could sit and relax like two normal people; they could sit and drink tea and talk to each other quite naturally and she would get to know something more about him — this strange and attractive young man who was still so much of a mystery.

But she was wrong.

The tea made and poured into two white china mugs, Gareth took his to the far end of the kitchen, where he sat on a stool, his heels hooked over the wooden bar close to the base. He held the mug in both hands and drank from it quickly, keeping perfect silence in the pauses. Jane drank her own tea, uncertain how to break the silence, finally not being able to do so at all.

'Thanks for the tea.' He rinsed his mug swiftly in the sink, gave Jane a raking glance as he stepped past, and closed the door firmly behind him.

The air seemed to hum for moments afterwards with his presence. She could feel the closeness of his arm, the intensity of his stare, could feel – almost – the warmth of his breath on her mouth, her nose, her face. When the door opened again, she jumped and the mug came close to falling from her hands.

'Martin McCabe,' said the woman in the tweed suit, 'did you find out . . . '

'A quarter to three,' Jane replied, holding her voice steady. 'If his train's on time he should be here by a quarter to three.'

Jane was in the office typing a letter to her friend Maggie when she heard the car on its way down the hill. There was just time to finish her paragraph explaining (or *trying* to explain) to Maggie about the peculiar feelings which had arisen from her encounters with Gareth, before hurrying out on to the flat stones of the yard.

She glimpsed another face through the windscreen alongside her father's and presumed that this was their visiting poet – chosen from fifty or so applicants for a two-month residency at the centre, where he would spend some time teaching but be left free otherwise to continue his own work.

Jane watched as her father opened one door and waited for the aging silver-haired Scottish bard to extricate himself from the other.

First a dark leather bag was hoisted on to the car roof, swiftly followed by another, smaller but matching; these were joined by a portable typewriter in a glossy red case and finally their owner.

'Jane, this is Martin McCabe. Martin, this is my daughter Jane.'

Jane's mouth opened as she gazed at a young man with fair hair that had been cut so that it stood several inches off the crown of his head before bending a few degrees to the side. Blue eyes: a smile that came naturally and quickly and turned the edges of his mouth upwards into a grin. He left his luggage on the car roof and came towards where Jane was standing. He was wearing dark grey cotton trousers with a pleated waist, a soft grey shirt and a deep-red padded jacket that was tight where it was fastened above the hips.

'It's nice to meet you.' His grin changed back to a smile again and Jane realized he wasn't just holding her hand, he was squeezing it. 'Your father's talked about you practically all the way from the station.'

Jane glanced towards Richard to reproach him and as she did so, Martin McCabe moved close enough to kiss her swiftly on the cheek.

'Anything else about you,' he said, 'I'll have to find out for myself.'

And he lifted his luggage clear of the car and followed Richard into the house, leaving Jane in his wake. She stood where she was, going over in her mind what had just happened, trying to establish the events clearly, doing her best to remember exactly what he had said – shaking her head as she realized just how wrong about him she had been. An elderly Scotsman with white hair and a pipe, indeed! So much for her imagination!

She thought about going into the house after them, but decided against it. There was still her letter to Maggie to finish and now she had even more news to tell. She was almost at the office door when something made her turn her head: at the far end of the yard, close to the wall and the gate, stood Gareth. He was watching her now, exactly as she understood he had been watching Martin's arrival.

The held hand.

The smiling words.

The kiss on the cheek.

She didn't know whether she was glad that Gareth had seen them or not. For a moment she tried to read his expression, but since she couldn't do that from less than an arm's length away, what chance had she from forty yards?

Jane turned her back on Gareth and closed the door behind her. She sat at the desk and moved the carriage back to the beginning of a new line.

Maggie, you'll never guess what just happened . . .

Chapter 8

The wind caught at Jane's hair and tugged at it play-fully. Above her a pair of larks fluttered and sang, the piping music of their notes rippling away in the air. She turned and looked back the way she had come, arms folded across her chest. The dark line that marked the stone wall over which she had clambered was now at the edge of her vision. There was no longer either sign or sense of what lay below: everything was the tops, the moor. Earth and heather stretched from beneath her feet. The sky seemed to press down on her, so close that if she could only reach high enough . . .

Jane watched as the sun shone from the jagged sur-faces of the crags, a shifting pattern of reflections that danced as she walked towards it.

. . . bare masses of stone, with hardly enough earth in their clefts to nourish a stunted tree.

Alone there with only the sun and wind, Jane felt an exultation that was different from anything she had known before. She felt for the first time that she might begin truly to understand this wild landscape, to be more than simply another admiring stranger. And yet . . . She fingered the lens cap from the front of her camera and raised it to her eye, adjusting the focus as she did so. And yet, if she was ever to be more than an admiring stranger, why was she behaving as one? Why was she taking pictures, like any other visitor, any other tourist?

The answer came clearly as her finger pressed down lightly but evenly upon the shutter: she was a photographer. That was what she did, what she loved, what she always wanted to do. And if there was something about these topmost heights which she could capture in a way that so many others had not, then her relationship with them would be different. Special. In those pictures they would be *her* heights, just as Emily Brontë had taken Pennistone Crags and made them her own.

. . . among the heather on those hills . . .

Jane leant back against the rock and rewound the film inside her camera; she had another film in her pocket and now that the light was beginning to fade a little the atmosphere was changing. She would capture it as best she could. Perhaps if she climbed higher on the crags, up where the last scrawny tree held out against the buffeting of the wind . . .

She slotted one foot into a convenient crack and felt for hand-holds; her camera hung at her back so as not to swing forward and bang against the rock. From the top she would get a wonderful view, unimpeded across the moor, the sun beginning to slide down towards the folded hills on the horizon.

She climbed steadily now, pausing only to catch her

breath. Just a few more minutes and she would be there. Just . . .

As Jane's hand touched the bare face of the rock, here deeply ridged, there smooth and still warm from the sun, her blood froze. Another hand, another set of fingers touched her own. Automatically, her eyes jammed tight shut and she felt herself being hoisted through the air. Her knee banged against a ledge as she toppled forward; a cry fell from her lips and strong hands steadied her and held her still. When she looked she was standing at the summit of the rock and yet in a small hollow, a space carved out by generations of wind and rain. Gareth looked into her face, studying her; then, as if suddenly realizing that he was still holding her arms, he drew his hands away and let his arms come back to his sides. ·

'You frightened the life out of me.'

'I'm sorry.'

'Why didn't you say something?'

'For a long time I didn't think you'd get all the way to the top.'

'And you would have let me go back without knowing you were here?'

'Why shouldn't I?'

Jane didn't know the answer: not for certain. Since the afternoon Gareth had witnessed the arrival of Martin McCabe, he had kept out of her way. There had been no cups of tea in the kitchen; he had ceased materializing in doorways at the very time that she had come to look for him. And so she had begun to talk with Martin instead. Unlike the first impression the poet had given her, he was not the brashly confident person he had appeared to be. True, he was certain about his writing, positive that he wanted above all else to be a poet – just as she was sure herself that she wanted to be a photographer. But at later meetings he was calmer, more gentle; there were times when he would sit silently, gazing off into space as if waiting for images to rise up in his mind so that he could capture them with his words. Show me, she had urged, show me what you're writing now. All Martin had done was to smile and shake his head and say that it wasn't ready to be looked at by anyone – not even by her.

'When it's ready,' he had said, 'you'll be the first to read it. I promise you.'

And, just as he had on that first day, Martin had taken her hand and for a brief moment squeezed it so that the pressure of his fingers was firm and warm against her own.

'So how come you're by yourself?' Gareth asked, leaning back against the rock.

'I've walked on my own ever since we arrived.'

Gareth's dark eyes seemed to be mocking her. 'I thought now it would be different.'

'I don't understand.'

'Yes, you do.'

Jane knew what he was thinking, what he was getting at; instinctively, she had felt his disapproval over what he imagined was going on between Martin and herself. She had known it from his absence.

'Nothing to say, then?'

She looked at him and held his gaze. 'Not about what's my business.'

'Is it?'

'Yes.'

The strength of her answer seemed to take him by surprise. Probably, thought Jane, the girls from the village are too frightened of him to talk back. Whereas she knew she owed him no explanation: what she did and who she spent time with, those were her business and nobody else's.

'It isn't what you think,' she said.

'What's that, then?' A smile was coming to his eyes.

'What you're suggesting.'

'I didn't think I was suggesting anything.'

'Well, you were.'

'What about?'

'Martin and me.'

Gareth laughed. 'Oh, that. Why d'you think I'd bother myself with that?'

Jane turned from his laughter; he was teasing her in his own way, playing games that she didn't quite understand. She reached towards the ledge.

'Going back, then?'

'Yes,' she said over her shoulder, beginning to climb down.

'Waiting for you, is he?'

'No!'

She glared at him angrily, her fingers pressing harder than necessary against the rock so that the rough edges cut against her skin.

'Always kiss people the first time you see them, do you?'

Jane flushed. 'No. And besides, I didn't kiss him, he kissed me.'

'Much the same,' said Gareth.

(No, it's not, thought Jane. Oh, no it's not.)

He reached down his hand until it was touching her shoulder. 'Sometimes it's best to wait. Till it means something.'

She knew that he was going to try and kiss her then. She saw the movement of his body, the lowering of his head, the dark flash of his eyes. She twisted from under his grasp and clambered down towards the ground, the sound of Gareth's laughter trailing mockingly behind her.

Chapter 9

The copy of *Wuthering Heights* was open on her lap but for once the story refused to draw her into itself; a mug of coffee was growing colder and colder at her side. Why did he have to be so stupid! So unreason-able! What was it about boys that made them all the same? Boys. Men. They all seemed capable of some strange kind of jealousy that knocked whatever common sense they might have possessed clear out of their heads.

She almost snorted at the memory of the expression on Gareth's face as he stood there and made his assertions about Martin. As if it was any business of his what was going on between the two of them – not that anything was.

Jane lifted the mug to her lips almost absent-mindedly. Martin McCabe. He was good-looking, she had to admit that. And intelligent. And he wore good clothes. Far more the sort of boy she was likely to be interested in than Gareth with his muddy and patched jeans, his scuffed boots and his thick hair that hadn't had a comb passed through it for more than a week.

A walking scarecrow, that's what he was!

'Ugh!' She swallowed the mouthful of lukewarm coffee with distaste and set it down again hastily, spilling a little of it on to her fingers.

Gareth's face was still there in her imagination, no matter how hard she might try to dismiss it. That movement towards her, as if going to kiss her, and then her own face twisting aside and ducking away.

Why?

Didn't she want to be kissed?

No, came the answer.

(But she had been kissed before – and by and large she had enjoyed it. There had been occasions on which she had considered it an over-rated pastime, but basically she was affirmative about kissing. Ever since that boy who had left school suddenly to become an acrobat had taken her hand and asked her to go for a walk in the car park during the fourth year disco.)

Then was it just that she didn't want to be kissed by Gareth?

Jane thought that one over for a moment or two, trying to imagine exactly what it would be like.

No, she lied to herself, she did not in the least want to be kissed by Gareth.

In which case, did the prospect of being kissed by Martin hold out any more charms? Or – since he had already given her a sort of kiss within seconds of meeting her – did she want to kiss him?

Jane closed her eyes and concentrated hard on the possibility.

She still had her eyes closed when someone coughed softly and discreetly behind her. She jumped and the book went skittering away across the floor of the kitchen. Martin stooped easily and retrieved it, glancing at the spine before he handed it back.

'Are you enjoying it?' There was a playful lilt in his voice, a smile in his eyes that suggested to Jane that he was teasing her, though she couldn't tell how or why.

'It's great!' She looked at him keenly. 'Don't you think so?'

Martin pulled one of the stools away from the side and sat down. 'It's got some smashing stuff in it, but . . .'

'But what?'

'But do you want another cup of coffee? That one looks rather the worse for wear.'

'But what about the book?'

'Well,' he said, stretching across for the electric kettle, 'I have problems with Heathcliff.'

'So did Catherine,' laughed Jane.

'That's exactly it. I can't quite see how any intelligent young woman could throw herself at a wild man like that.'

'She doesn't throw herself at him. She tries to get away from him.'

'Ah,' pronounced Martin meaningfully, spooning instant coffee into two red mugs.

'What's that supposed to mean?'

He grinned at her. 'Running away – isn't that the surest sign that you want something so much you're frightened of your feelings?'

Jane drew her knees tight to her chest, hands clenched over the fading denim of her jeans. The memory of earlier on the moors came back to her so vividly she could almost feel Gareth's hand on her shoulder and the burr of his voice in her ear. She saw again the movement of his body and the flash of his dark eyes as his head moved closer to hers.

When she looked up again, Martin was staring at her curiously.

'Am I right, then?'

'About what?' Jane asked, hoping that she wasn't about to give herself away by blushing.

'Running away from things you want.'

She shook her head and half-turned away and at that exact moment Gareth walked past the kitchen window. Jane's fingers clutched at the wood of the stool and she held her breath lest Gareth were to turn his head and look in her direction. *Their* direction. But he carried on towards the upper garden, spade slung over his shoulder, head lowered towards the ground. Whatever held him deep in thought, it kept his attention away from anything that was going on inside the house.

If Martin noticed Gareth pass by, he said nothing. Instead he handed Jane the fresh mug of coffee and sat back down with his own.

'Sugar?'

'No, thanks.'

'Biscuit?'

She shook her head. Martin took one, then two, from the tin and set them on one knee of his grey cotton trousers. As usual, Jane realized, he was far too smartly dressed to be up there on the edge of that wilderness. She wondered if he had ever been up on to the moors himself and if so whether he had all the correct gear for walking long distances. And if he wasn't going to venture forth far beyond the house, why had he come there to write his poetry? Didn't poets write about where they were and what was going on around them? Or was it always what was going on inside their heads?

'Why isn't your mother here?' His question was soft-spoken enough but still it startled her.

'I'm sorry . . .'

'I wondered why you had come with your father and not your mother. I mean . . .'

'They're divorced.'

'I see.' He dunked a biscuit and ate one section. 'I'm sorry.'

'It doesn't matter.'

They looked at each other for a moment, each knowing that Jane's last remark was less than the truth. Then Martin started to ask her what she had been studying in the sixth form and what she was going to do after Mill House and Jane soon found that she was talking to him easily, enjoying his company without any of the tension she had felt when she was with Gareth. For the second time, most of her coffee grew cold before she got around to drinking it: and only the occasional sounds from the terraced garden across the yard from the kitchen reminded her that Gareth was never far away.

That night Jane dreamt herself back into her childhood. She was thirteen, tucked underneath her duvet in the narrow bed she had shared for so long with two ragged teddy-bears and a real live cat with a black smudge on the side of its nose like a mistake.

In the depth of her dream she woke to the sound of voices and sat up in bed, listening. They were blurred, too much so for her to pick out the words, a man's voice and a woman's. Something about them turned her skin cold; her stomach clenched hard inside her. The hair began to prickle at the base of her neck.

Helen, I've told you . . .

Richard, you just aren't being reasonable . . .
If I'd been less reasonable and more truthful . . .
Truthful! Is that what you call it? Don't make me
laugh!

Jane pulled her knees up to her chest and pushed her head down against them, pressing both hands as hard as she could against her ears. She knew those voices, knew those words, those arguments. She could remember when she had heard them first, out there on the landing outside her room. She had jumped from the bed then and run to the door and hurled it open. The voices had stopped abruptly and her father and mother had been staring at her, astonished, as if in the heat of their quarrel they had forgotten she was there at all.

She remembered her father slamming his fist against the wall and coming fast towards her. Instinctively she had cowered back, afraid that in his temper he might strike her. Instead he had aimed a clumsy kiss at her face and run down the stairs three at a time. Before she had been able to realize fully what was happening the front door had been opened and slammed shut.

The bed that Jane woke into was wider and she didn't share it with anything — no cat, no teddy bears. It was a long time since those awful times had come back to haunt her. Angry words that echoed and refused to fade away. All that love turning to hate before her eyes. She asked herself if it was always like that: for everyone.

She slipped out of bed and stood by the window, gazing up into the darkness of the sky, the stars small and distant, high over the tops. And as she looked a cloud slid across the moon and left it uncovered, almost full and shining. She could just pick out the silhouettes of trees and, beyond them, the uneven edge of the stone wall that marked the beginning of the moor. For the merest moment, she imagined she saw a figure standing there, waiting. Waiting for her . . . to do what? . . . make up her mind?

The moment passed and the moon was covered once more by cloud.

Jane stared out into the darkness.

Heathcliff?

Gareth?

She shook her head and went back to bed. Within minutes she was fast asleep.

Chapter 10

She woke early next morning, pushed back the covers and went to the bathroom; less than ten minutes later, camera over her shoulder, she was outside. A haze hung between the trees like netting that had been artlessly draped there overnight: crystals of dew shone from webs trailing between blades of grass. A ring of orange light was close to the horizon as Jane climbed towards the moor. A knot of excitement twisted pleasurably in her stomach as she thought of the shots she would be able to take: close-ups using one lens, wide-angled panoramas of dawn with another. The ground was damp beneath her feet and she paused for a moment to button her padded black jacket and pull its collar high against her neck.

She had been walking, taking pictures for almost an hour when she suddenly sensed rather than saw that she was no longer alone. There he was, Gareth, walking close to a wall that led away from her own path at right angles. His hands were in his pocket and he moved slowly, thoughtfully; anyone else might have considered that he had not seen her, but Jane was certain that he had.

She half-wanted to call out to him, almost did, but some uncertainty – a fear almost – prevented her. She could not be sure of how he would react and the last thing she wanted was to provoke him. If he wanted to speak to her again, he would do so in his own good time.

She turned away, walked another fifty yards, and then focused her camera upon the stack of the first mill chimney as it poked above the slowly dispersing haze.

She changed her angle several times before making the shot and by the time it was done, Gareth was nowhere to be seen.

When she had come to the end of her film and checked

her watch it was close to eight. Her father would be up and about and breakfast would be ready. She let herself imagine she could smell the fresh coffee all the way from the house.

Moving her camera strap, so that the Pentax hung from one shoulder, she climbed over the wall and started towards the narrow track that would lead her home. She had scarcely started down the track when she noticed Gareth standing close against a tree, hands in the pockets of his jeans, staring at the ground.

She could have left the path and carried on down through the bracken, but she didn't want to: it would have been giving in, making more of his presence than she actually felt. She didn't want to let Gareth think that she was in any way scared of him, whatever else he might think. After all, if he wanted to pose about like that, all moody and glowering, that was his affair!

But when she got closer, Gareth's head came up and he wasn't looking moody at all; he even managed a quick smile.

'I'm sorry,' he said, his tone suggesting that he meant it.

'Whatever for?'

'Yesterday. I was being stupid.'

'Not really.'

'Yes, I was. I suppose I'm not used to . . . ' His words faltered to nothing and it was just his dark eyes looking at her.

'Not used to what?' Without exactly meaning to, Jane had moved closer to where Gareth was standing.

Close enough to rest her hand against the trunk of the tree.

'Girls like you.'

Jane laughed. 'What's so different about me?'

The seriousness of his answer cut her laughter short. 'You're lovely. Clever . . . '

'No, I'm . . . '

'You're not like any girl I've ever met.'

His hand grasped the tree, fingers hard against the bark and no more than six inches above her own. Neither of them was going to say anything now. She held her breath as his hand came closer; the first contact almost made her pull her fingers away as though a charge had leaped through them. But then his hand was covering hers, his other arm moved towards her and drew her to him. Not roughly, never harshly: there was no more anger, no trace of mockery. Her own free hand was round his neck and she was touching the warmth of his dark skin, sliding her fingers through the curls of his hair.

When he kissed her she wanted to open her eyes and look at him but somehow she couldn't. He held her so tight against him that it was difficult to breathe.

'Gareth!'

'What?' He pulled his head away, still holding her close. One of Jane's hands was pressed against him, between shoulder and chest, keeping him off.

'You're squeezing me to death!'

The smile came slowly from his eyes, more quickly to the edges of his mouth. When he kissed her a second time it was slower, more gentle; she moved her hand away and this time she did open her eyes. Gareth's were closed and she could see the thickness of his long, dark lashes as his mouth moved over hers.

Jane felt as though something was churning her around inside, some feeling that she was unused to. She placed one hand against Gareth's shoulder and moved him away.

'What is it?'

'Nothing.'

'Shouldn't I have done that?'

She smiled. 'Of course you should. If you wanted to.'

'I've been wanting to for ages,' he said and then wished that he hadn't. 'But then I expect you know that.'

'Do I?' Jane asked, half teasing.

'Girls like you.'

'What does that mean?' she asked, ready to be offended.

'You know, city girls, sophisticated . . .'

Jane laughed; she couldn't help it.

'See what I mean.'

'No.'

'Well, you're laughing at me, aren't you?'

She shook her head. 'I'm laughing at the idea of my being sophisticated.'

A hush fell between them and neither moved or spoke. She thought she wanted Gareth to kiss her again, not certain even now that she could recall exactly what it had been like. The force and suddenness of it had scarcely given her time to concentrate on what was happening. With someone else she might have put her arms round him and made it clear what she wanted, but not with Gareth. It was going to take more than this to let her feel at ease in his company.

'Are you going back down?' Gareth asked, leaning back against the nearest tree and picking at one of the branches.

'Umm. Breakfast. How about you?'

He shook his head. 'I've got to go back into the village.'

'Oh.'

Silence again. Gareth broke off one twig and then another; Jane traced patterns in the dry earth with her toe.

'Do you want to go for a walk at lunchtime?' she asked finally, needing to break the quiet and not wanting simply to say goodbye.

'All right. I can take an hour.'

'Me too.' Jane began to move off down the track. 'See you at one then. At the gate past the house.'

Gareth nodded, jammed his hands back into his pockets and headed off through the trees.

'Up early,' Richard remarked as she came into the cottage.

'I wanted to take some pictures,' she explained, lifting the camera away and setting it down on the table by the toast and the pots of jam and marmalade.

Richard's head was back in yesterday's paper. 'Get what you wanted?'

'Yes,' Jane said, pouring herself some coffee. 'Yes. At least, I think so.'

'Hmm,' said her father, 'I suppose you'll have to wait and see how things develop.'

She turned to look at his face, just in case he was getting at something more than photography. But he was more interested in the cricket scores than anything else.

Jane was buttering her second piece of toast when Richard said, 'I may be a bit late back from lunch. I said I'd pop into the village for a chat. One of the locals with a few questions about the place. You'll be okay, won't you?'

She looked at him and nodded. I'll be fine, she thought. Just fine.

Gareth was waiting at the gate at one sharp. Without discussion they walked down the valley and he began to ask her questions, more or less the same ones that Martin had asked, except the phrases were less cultured and his tone lacked any sense of irony. He simply wanted to know about her and, as simply as she could, she told him.

When she told him about her parents' separation, he stopped and looked at her, anger shining in his eyes.

'Why come here with him then?'

'My father?'

'Who else?'

'Why shouldn't I?'

'After he walked out on you like that?'

'He didn't walk out on me.'

'On your mother, then. It's the same thing.'

'No, it isn't.'

Gareth started to walk briskly away. 'To me it is,' he said over his shoulder.

She had to run to catch up with him; there were questions she wanted to ask him now, but she was hesitant about it.

'Gareth,' she said five minutes later, as they stopped in a clearing, pigeons breaking through the tall branches overhead and whirring away.

'What is it?'

'Did something happen with your father?'

At first she thought he wasn't going to answer. Then he bunched his hands into fists and glared down at them. 'When I was ten he walked out on us. We've never seen him since. Not my sisters, my brother, my mother or me. And if I ever do see him again, I'll kill him.'

'Gareth! Don't say that!'

'Why not? It's true.'

Jane saw all the hurt showing through that fierce anger and thought for the first time that she understood something about him. She moved close to him and took his hands in hers and waited until they were fists no longer; with his fingers locked in hers, she moved her mouth to his and kissed him softly, letting herself feel the sensation, not wanting to forget, this time, what it was like.

They walked on through the trees, holding hands now, lapsed into a silence that was less uncomfortable than before, though she could tell that Gareth was still thinking about his own father. How lucky she was to know that Richard still loved her, she thought; no matter what had happened between her mother and himself, he had hardly ever given her occasion to doubt that.

Ten minutes later, they turned round and, the sun breaking through the trees on to their backs, headed back towards the house.

Chapter 11

'Let's go down to the river,' Jane said once the house was in sight. 'I don't want to go back yet.'

Gareth nodded and they skirted round the wall, cutting across to the lower path. Jane didn't know if she wanted to go back into the yard holding Gareth's hand, making some kind of announcement to anyone who might be there to see them. She didn't know if she wanted that – not yet. Not to be seen by her father, by Martin . . .

The path twisted sharply to the left, through the back yard of a farmer's cottage, then turned at right angles upon itself before dropping down to the valley bottom.

Gareth let go of her hand and put one arm around

her shoulders instead. Jane reached up and slid her fingers through his. They were like this when they saw they were no longer alone: there were people down on the bridge. Three of them – a man, a woman and a small child. A family group.

Jane and Gareth watched as the man lifted the child aloft and then sat him on the parapet of the curved bridge, his legs dangling over the trickling water. Then they saw him lift the woman also and whirl her once around, the sound of their laughter mingling as it rose upwards. The man set the woman down and kissed the top of her head, her eyes, cheeks, finally her mouth.

The kiss seemed to go on for a long time.

A long time.

Jane's legs were weak, her stomach was empty, a vacuum that nevertheless knotted and tightened fast. She leant her weight against Gareth but then spun away.

Down on the bridge the couple had stopped kissing. They held hands for a moment or two, arms angled downwards, before the man swung the child back off the bridge and set him down between them. They walked on over the bridge, each holding one of the child's hands, lightly swinging his arms, away on to the far side of the valley.

Jane stood where she was, unable to move. Thoughts raced round in her brain, chasing one another until they tumbled into a blur of meaning that she couldn't, didn't want to understand.

Gareth set one hand on her arm and she spun away, arching her body backwards like an animal.

'No!' she hissed.

'Jane . . .'

'No!'

And she turned on her heels and began to run, heedlessly, neither knowing nor caring where she was going. Her legs raced through the bracken, she dodged between bushes, skirted trees, threw up her arms to shield her face from branches that hung across her path. At first she thought she could hear Gareth coming after her, but after a while there was only the sound of her own crashing progress and of her breath rasping from her lungs.

A stitch bit high into her left side, hard against her ribs. She rubbed at it as she continued to run, stumbling now, her legs beginning to weaken. Her feet slithered on old leaves and she grabbed at a branch to keep herself from falling headlong.

Within moments she burst into the clearing around the first of the old mill chimneys and threw herself to the ground. On her back and gasping for breath, she stared up through the overhanging trees and followed the chimney's climb towards the now darkening sky.

All she could see was the scene from the bridge, replaying itself over and over in her mind: her father, so happy, swinging first the child and then the woman in his arms – her father kissing the woman fully, lovingly, just as, minutes earlier, Gareth had been kissing her.

Jane drew her knees close to her chest and clasped her legs tightly and then, at last, the tears came. Tears, loud and unceasing, until her body ached with the sheer, racking pain of them. On and on and on.

It was dark. The stonework was coarse against her back, sending a cold dampness spreading through her. The ends of her fingers were growing numb; she had lost all feeling in her toes. She tried to remember how long ago she had moved inside the chimney, but time seemed to have lost any meaning for her. Now and again, a rustling through the valley floor outside would startle her, make her pulse beat a shade faster. Once she thought she heard an owl but realized that she didn't truly know what an owl sounded like.

Her thoughts circled and landed, circled and landed, ever and ever around the same moments, the same movements. Always her father's arms reaching out: always the pleasure on his face, unmistakable even from a distance: again and again, the sound of his laughter.

Why had he never said?

Never as much as hinted.

Why, oh why had he never warned her?

Of course, when her parents had first split up and it had become obvious they would not get back together again, Jane's thoughts had been tormented by the fact that her father had fallen in love with another woman. She had dreaded being told that he was living with someone else, that he would remarry after the divorce, that there would be a new family, one which would exclude her from its centre. But the news she had been so frightened of had never arrived. If her father saw other women – and she didn't think of him as having become a monk overnight; after all he was an attractive man – she saw no sign of them. And so she supposed that there was no one serious in his life, no romance.

What a fool she had been!

Sitting there, huddled in the dark, Jane tried to reconstruct the woman's face. Dark hair, a wide face, a young face – much younger than her father, she was sure of that. And the child. Hers, certainly, but hers and her father's? Jane rocked forwards and back, her head touching the cold stone with each movement. A shiver ran through the curve of her body. More sounds rustled and shimmered outside. She closed her eyes and gave way to her worst imaginings.

Torchlight flickered across the clearing, faded an instant, then settled on the stonework of the chimney base, sliding carefully round, seeking out the entrance. The sliver of light pierced the deep blackness of the interior, swung backwards again, then forwards, always getting nearer, always searching.

Boots crunched dry leaves into the hardness of cold earth.

For seconds only Jane's face was trapped in an oval of brightness.

Then Gareth's body was hunched down alongside

her own, his arms close about her, careful not to hold her too tight, not to let any of his own fear find its way through to her.

For some minutes neither of them spoke.

He set the torch on the ground and flicked it back on, making sure that it was pointing away, spooling out across the floor and the wall opposite. Gareth squatted in front of Jane and ran his fingers down the sides of her face, smooth and cold as the gravestone marble that stood between the twin churches of the village. He found her hands and rubbed them briskly with his own, encouraging her circulation, bringing her warmth.

'Are you all right?' His voice, when it came, echoed oddly in the enclosed space.

Jane nodded. A sound came falteringly from her lips which might have been a yes.

'Everyone was worried about you. I was worried about you. When you ran off I thought maybe it was best to leave you to yourself, but then when you didn't come back . . . '

'Did you tell . . . ? My father, does he know?' Her voice was strained and cracked; it seemed to belong to somebody she didn't really know.

'He's out looking for you now. And some of the others.' He paused. 'Martin.'

Jane let her head fall against Gareth's chest. 'I'm glad you found me.'

How long it was before Gareth tried to get her to

stand, Jane didn't know. The numbness had spread through her body and her legs were stiff and stung with pins and needles when she put her weight on them. It was all she could do to stand with Gareth supporting her – several minutes like that before she began to limp towards the entrance.

'You sure you don't want to wait here? I can find one of the others and between us we could carry you.'

'No. No. I'll be all right. As long as we take it slowly. I'd rather it was like this.'

What she meant was, I want it to take as long as possible before we get back, as long as possible before I have to face my father.

The lights were on in the cottage and the door was unlatched but there was nobody there. Gareth steered Jane to a chair and then went into the little kitchen and put on the kettle. He looked for a bottle of brandy, found some whisky and forced a glass into her hands.

'He'll be back soon, don't worry. They know at the house where you are.'

Jane's eyes closed, partly through exhaustion, partly to shut out what she knew must happen; the confrontation she had run away from.

She sipped some of the whisky and almost choked it back. Steps sounded on the stones outside. The door was flung back and her father was standing there, strain lining his face, making him older than Jane had ever seen him.

'There's tea in the pot,' said Gareth, stepping round Richard and closing the door at his back.

Father and daughter stared at each other without moving.

Chapter 12

Silence gathered between them. Neither Jane nor her father moved. On the mantelshelf, the old clock clicked the minutes past. One of the cats – she didn't see which – tried to jump up on to Jane's lap and she lifted it back down.

'I was . . .' The words came with difficulty, Richard's face still creased with worry and regret. 'We were . . . worried. Worried sick. About you. It's so . . .' He moved from the doorway, one, two short paces, hesitated, took one more. 'After dark, it's so easy to get lost. And if you'd gone up on to the moor . . .'

His eyes closed as if to shut out the thought.

Jane wanted to go to him and hold him, tell him that it was all right. Part of her. But something else still held her back. Just as her father was trapped inside a vision of his daughter as a frozen, huddled mass on the exposed heights, so Jane couldn't yet free herself from that picture of perfect happiness in the afternoon sunlight on the bridge – a picture that excluded her, kept her outside its frame.

'We called the police. Volunteers from the village. Another hour and . . . '

'Dad.'

'Yes?'

'It doesn't matter now. I'm here. I know I shouldn't have caused everyone so much worry. I'm sorry – but talking about it won't make any difference.'

Richard almost smiled. 'It might to me. All that time searching for you, I couldn't say a thing. I suppose I was terrified that if I said what I was thinking out loud that might make it happen.'

'Well, it didn't. Isn't that the important thing?'

He did smile then; he came over to where Jane was sitting and reached down towards her and took her in his arms. For several minutes they sat like that, each safe in the other's closeness. Jane knew that her father was crying, knew that she wanted to cry herself but that for now she had left her tears in those lonely hours of isolation as darkness and silence had settled around her.

'Listen,' Richard pulled back, wiping at his face with his hand, grinning now through what was left of his tears, 'if we don't do something about that tea, it's going to be so stewed you'll be able to stand the spoon up in it.'

'I thought that was how you liked it,' Jane smiled.

He laughed and went into the kitchen. Jane stood and surveyed her face in the round mirror above the fireplace: she looked dreadful! Seeing her like that would have knocked any thoughts about how lovely she was from Gareth's head. Gareth: she hadn't really thanked him properly. And she had been so glad that he had been the one to find her, not some policeman or climber whom she had never seen before.

'Here we go.'

Richard moved the small, round table between them with his foot, set the cups down, went back for biscuits and slices of cake.

'Are you sure you're warm enough?'

'Fine.'

'You wouldn't like a hot water bottle or something? A blanket?'

'Dad, I said. I'm okay.'

'I just don't want you to come down with a chill, that's all.'

They sat there and drank their tea, her father dunking the occasional biscuit, neither saying anything of importance. The clock continued to click its way round loudly, reminding each of them that all they were doing was putting off the inevitable.

Finally Richard put his cup down into its saucer with deliberation and sat back forcefully in his chair. 'All right.'

She looked at him expectantly.

'There's something I want to show you.'

He went and fetched his wallet, opening it as he came back to the chair. On the table in front of Jane he set three photographs. She knew what she would see almost before her eyes had shifted focus.

A young woman stood in open space, a wooden cabin behind her. She was wearing walking boots, long and thick white socks, dark trousers and a white sweater. Her dark hair was partly hidden under a white woollen hat. She was looking directly at the camera and smiling – no, more than smiling. Glowing: that was the word for it. Glowing with happiness.

In the second picture, slightly out of focus, the same woman was standing in a street somewhere. Her hands were pushed down into the pockets of a hip-length coat; a red scarf wound about her neck. She wasn't looking at the camera this time, rather she was turning away as if she didn't want the photograph to be taken. There was no sign of pleasure, of happiness on her face.

The third photo was small and square, the kind you take in cubicles at railway stations or post offices. A young boy's face half-smiled lopsidedly at the camera, his mouth open and his head to one side. His hair was dark and quite long, covering his ears. He looked just like his mother.

Jane stared down until the images began to blur, the one into the other.

At first Richard's voice seemed to come from nowhere, as if Jane in her concentration on the photos had forgotten he was there.

'Her name is Karen. And the little boy, her son, he's named Peter. Pete.'

Jane's head twisted towards him and her words were quick and angry. 'And you? What are they to you? What . . . ?'

Richard took one of her hands and held it tight.

'I know. I should have told you before. I should have told you so many times, and so many times I almost did but I couldn't force the words out of my mouth.' He let go of her hand and for a moment looked away towards the darkness pressing up against the window. 'If somehow I'd found the courage to do that, today would never have happened.'

He shook his head, sighed, glanced down at the pictures, remembering.

'Five, almost six years ago, I was working in Manchester. It was only temporary, I didn't know anybody there. All the usual things, I suppose. Your mother and I hadn't been getting on and whenever I phoned her there was a chill on the line that made me feel even further away than I was. I'm not saying whose fault that was, there's no point in talking now about blame, though I like to think it isn't all mine.

'Anyway, that was when I met Karen. She was working in the office next to mine, we got to know each other a little: five minutes here, five minutes there. One day I went into an Italian restaurant, a café really, just for lunch and she was sitting at a table, finishing her coffee. After that, I don't know, it simply happened. She was so easy to talk to, she wanted to know about what I was doing, about my life . . . '

'You told her you were married?' interrupted Jane.

'Of course I did. And about you – I must have bored her silly talking about you.'

(Maybe, thought Jane, you should have been talking *to* me instead.)

90

What she said was: 'And knowing you were married, that didn't make any difference to her? This, what was her name?' (As if she could ever forget her name!) 'Karen.'

'You're trying to make her something she's not.' The signs of anger were clear at the base of Richard's voice.

'Am I?'

'Yes! Yes.' Richard sighed, clenched his hands, unclenched them, sighed again. 'You've got to understand . . .'

'Got to . . . ?'

'Jane, it wasn't like that.'

'Oh, really?'

'What I mean is, at first, for a long time, well . . . neither of us realized what was happening. We thought – oh, I don't know what we thought. Maybe we didn't think at all.'

(Very likely! Jane thought.)

'It was different, something apart. It didn't seem to have anything to so with you or your mother.'

'You mean you forgot all about us.'

'No! . . . Yes. Yes. When I was with Karen I forgot about the pain your mother and I were causing each other; the pain I was causing you. And then one day . . . one morning . . . I was walking along the street to work and this bus went past and I saw Karen's face at the window. I remember that I started running towards the stop and, as soon as she appeared on the platform, calling her name. She came along the pavement to meet me and I knew from her face that she'd realized the same thing at the same time. I still don't know why it was, but just at that moment, that glimpse of her face blurring past, going away from me – I knew that I was in love with her.'

It seemed darker than before inside the small room, with only the small lamp in the corner switched on. Jane looked at the unclear outline of her father's face, trying to see things as he had seen them, feel as he had felt. But the picture she had in her mind of a young woman's face at one window kept merging with that of a young man with unruly hair, Gareth's face at another.

'What happened?' Jane asked.

Richard shook his head. 'Everything. Nothing. We saw each other as much as we could, spent every possible minute together, knowing that soon my job there would be finished and I would have to go back to Nottingham.'

'Back home.'

'Yes.'

'But if you were as much in love with her as you said?'

'I know. I know. Believe me, I still don't get through as much as a day when I don't hate myself for not doing what I should have done then. What happened to your mother and me was already going to happen. There was no way we were going to get back to the way we'd been. Staying in the same house all that time after I came back only made things worse; more difficult for us ever to trust each other again.'

'Then why didn't you tell her?'

Richard pushed himself up from the chair and walked to the door, to the window, back to the chair again. He stood with both arms stretched down, hands gripping the back of the fabric.

'I was too frightened. Too scared. To be honest. To tell your mother. To tell you. And – I suppose – there was always something somewhere at the back of my mind nagging at me, asking are you sure this is it, are you sure this is what you want for the rest of your life?'

'But wasn't it?'

'Yes! Oh, God, yes.'

'Then . . . ?'

Richard gestured vaguely with his hands. 'What terrified me – one of the things – the worst thing – I knew what I'd felt when your mother and I got married, how much we loved each other then and when we had you. And yet I knew that had faded, died. I didn't want to go through that again.'

'And did you tell her all this? Karen, I mean.'

'I tried.'

'Then why didn't she understand?'

'She tried to.'

'Then she should have waited.'

Richard looked at Jane, surprised at the strength of her remark. 'Jane, she did wait, believe me. Waited through endless letters and phone calls and visits snatched whenever I could arrange them. Once we managed a weekend in the Lakes. That's where that picture was taken. It was probably the best time we had together, the closest. We walked until our legs and feet ached, talked until we were hoarse, made all kinds of plans. I was going to go back and tell your mother I wanted a divorce, explain about Karen . . . we even talked about having children of our own, everything.'

There was another moment of silence between them and this time it was Jane who reached across and took her father's hands between her own.

'And you didn't do it,' she said quietly, sadly.

'No.' His voice was almost unheard in the dimly lit room. 'No. Not then. Not until your mother forced it out of me. And by then it was too late.'

'Why?'

'Why?' Richard laughed: a laugh empty of anything but bitterness. 'Karen had met somebody else.'

'But if she loved you . . . '

'Her loving me wasn't in question. What she couldn't be sure of was how much I loved her. One day I was promising all kinds of things, the next we were still apart. And suddenly there was this other man saying all of the things I'd been saying but apparently meaning them more, doing something about them. A man who would marry her.'

'But she was younger than you. She could have waited.'

Richard squeezed her hands. 'Being young . . . maybe that was why she couldn't wait.'

They looked at each other until Richard leant over and kissed Jane on the forehead.

'I'm sorry, Dad. Really, no matter what else I might feel. I hate to see you so miserable.'

He got to his feet, lifting Jane after him. 'I'm not. Most of the time. Not now. You know I'm not.' Turning to the side, he switched on the main light. 'See . . . ' widening his face into an artificial smile ' . . . I'm happy. I am most of the time. Especially now I've got this job. You're here with me and I haven't got time to think about being miserable.'

'Only today . . . ' Jane began.

'Karen was on her way to Lancaster. That's where they live. She rang, we'd always kept that much in touch, knowing where we were. She said did I want to see her, did I want to see her son? Their son. I'd only seen a photo – that one there.'

'Wouldn't it have been better to have said no?'

Richard shrugged. 'For you, probably, though you'd have found out sooner or later, one way or another.'

'And you?'

'Once I knew the chance of seeing her was there . . . I couldn't say no. And I did want to see Pete. She'd talked about him and . . . '

'You still phone her?' asked Jane, surprised.

'She rings me. Not often. Once every couple of months. To see if I'm still okay, I suppose.'

'It must hurt a lot.'

'It's better than never knowing where she is, what she's doing, how she is.'

'And is she happy?'

'I think so.' For a moment he closed his eyes. 'I hope so.'

Jane put her arms round him and gave him a hug. He looked tired out whereas she seemed to have forgotten about the hours she had spent alone and cold and feeling sorry for herself. There were, she now realized, others with greater cause for self-pity than she.

'I'm hungry,' she said briskly, moving towards the kitchen. 'How about baked beans?'

'On toast?'

'Of course.'

'With grated cheese on top?'

'Naturally.'

'How about an egg mixed in?'

'What else?'

'Er . . . a few drops of tabasco sauce?'

'Sorry, there isn't any.'

'Paprika?'

'No.'

'Cayenne pepper?'

'Think again.'

'Mustard?'

'Mustard we've got.'

'Want me to help?'

'Nope. You can wash up.'

Richard grinned and flopped down into the easy chair. Now that it was out, now that he'd said it all, it was as if a weight had been lifted from his shoulders, one he hadn't fully realized was there. While out in the kitchen, slicing thick pieces of bread, Jane was thinking that she was closer now to her father than she had ever been before. More than that, she had learned something, learned a lot. And she hoped that nobody would ever be able to say of her that she had acted too impulsively because she had been too young to know any better.

Chapter 13

Martin was sitting in a deck chair at the front of the house, his legs angled upwards so that his bare feet were resting against the upper section of railings. He was wearing light green cords, a white short-sleeved shirt with its sleeves folded back once and the collar turned up at the neck. A Sony Walkman was clipped to the left side of his belt and the headphones, red circles at the end of polished metal, were held fast to the sides of his head. He had a notebook open in his lap and a green felt-tip in the fingers of his right hand; three other pens – red, blue and yellow – rested within reach on the grass.

Lines of slanting red writing, slanting back upon itself, ran across the upper half of the page. Here and there words had been crossed out and others written over the top or in the margin – corrections in yellow and blue. All around the border of the writing a trellis work of leaves and vines had been carefully drawn in green, some of the leaves filled in, others left as outline.

Martin's head was moving lightly, side to side with the music that Jane could only imagine.

She had two cans of Coke, frosted cold from the fridge, one in each hand. Still unnoticed by Martin, she held one between her thighs while she pulled the top from the other and held it in front of his face.

Martin blinked and looked round, smiling.

Jane smiled back and opened her own can. 'Cheers!' she said, holding the Coke level with her face.

'Cheers!' boomed Martin, unnaturally loudly due to the volume of the music he was listening to.

When Jane laughed he realized what had happened and plucked the headphones from his head and let them rest on his writing pad. Tinny sound and a faint bass thud trickled out across the garden.

'I thought you might like something cold,' Jane said, sitting cross-legged on the ground beside the chair. 'It must be the hottest day of the year.'

'Since I've been here anyway,' Martin agreed.

After a few moments Jane gestured towards the pad with her can. 'How's it going?'

Martin made a face as if he were about to throw up.

'I bet it's not that bad.'

'You haven't seen it.'

'Are you going to let me?'

He shook his head.

'Why not?'

'Later.'

'When?' she asked, head to one side.

He grinned. 'When it's better.'

She lay back on the grass, holding the Coke can against the buckle of her jeans belt. 'I used to write poems. Dreadful things I scribbled in my diary up in my room. Real torchlight under the blankets stuff.' She shuddered. 'I'd just hate to see them now.'

'Maybe they were better than you think,' Martin offered.

'Worse, I expect. It was the sort of thing most young girls write. Drivel.'

Martin swung his legs down from the railings. 'I've done some work in schools. Given half the chance most kids can write terrific stuff – girls and boys. Really great. I wish I could write with such fluency. Half a line and I get stuck: too scared to put another word down, sometimes, in case it's the wrong one.'

They sat there for a while, drinking Coke and looking out over the field that dipped down into the valley. From the house there came the occasional sound of typewriters being pecked at cautiously with two fingers, the subdued noise of earnest conversation, now and then a burst of stifled laughter.

'I suppose I only wrote poems when I was miserable,' Jane said.

'It's as good a reason as any. It might not guarantee good poetry but it can help the person writing it.' He turned and looked at her seriously. 'Maybe if you were still writing poems you wouldn't be running off and getting lost.'

As soon as the words were out of his mouth he wished he'd never said them. 'I'm sorry. I shouldn't have . . . '

Jane raised a hand to stop him. 'It's okay. You're right. It was a childish thing to do.'

Martin shook his head. 'It's none of my business.'

'I don't mind talking about it.'

Martin smiled. 'I was out looking for you, you know. In the wrong place, of course.' He laughed. 'Probably as well – if I'd found you, then Gareth couldn't have.'

Jane felt herself flushing a little and swung her head away and concentrated on the view and finishing her Coke. When she sensed that Martin had gone back to his poem she sneaked a look at him. He really was a nice-looking young man. And the way he dressed was great. If she'd run into him back in Nottingham maybe things would have been different. Up here he was somehow out of place and although Jane was too, it didn't draw her to him. Instead it kept her at arm's length. Although, to be truthful, she didn't think he was interested in her – not in that kind of a way. Once upon a time she hadn't been able to tell if boys were interested in her and in what way, but as she'd gone through the sixth form her instinct had developed and nowadays she was usually right.

No, Martin would make a good considerate friend – maybe in time a close one – but nothing more.

At least, she didn't think so.

She got to her feet and shrugged her shoulders. 'I'll let you get back to your poem, then.'

'It's all right,' Martin said, but he didn't protest too much. She could tell that he wanted to get back to fighting it out with the words: literary warfare in four colours.

'See you later,' she said, moving away.

'Sure,' Martin grinned, and removed the top from his green pen. Before Jane had reached the door his headphones were back in place and rhythms were running back and forth inside his brain.

Chapter 14

After that night when he had discovered her and brought her back to the safety of the house, it was inevitable that a strong bond would exist between Jane and Gareth. He found more and more work to do in the gardens of the house, helping Richard now and again with other things that needed to be done inside the centre. And in breaks between these periods of work, or on days when there were no special visitors to the centre and Jane was free, they would walk across the moors and he would show her the special places that only he could find. Jane always had her camera with her and just as Gareth was opening up the countryside to her in a different way, so she did her best to capture that difference on film.

At first it didn't seem to be working. Her shots were no more special than the ones she had taken before. But then slowly, gradually, the hazy images which appeared and solidified in the developer were different, new; they were Gareth's moors and tops, but seen now through her eyes, making them different again – unique.

One evening after supper she spread them out on the table in front of her father and waited for his reaction.

'They're great! Fantastic! I didn't think anyone could do it.'

'Do what? Take pictures?'

'Take shots of these moors that didn't look the same as all the rest. But you've managed it. I don't know how, but what you've captured here – it's not the same. It's personal. It's you. I suppose that's what really good photography is – what makes it different from me wandering up there and taking snaps.'

'Yes. But a lot of it is Gareth as well. He was the one who showed me where to go, what to look at.'

'But he couldn't teach you how to get it on film. That's the art. That's you.'

She looked back at him, pleased, then down again at the pictures.

'I think what we should do,' Richard said, 'is make a

display of these inside the centre. After all, we do that for other people's work, why not yours?'

Jane smiled. 'All right. I'll make large prints and mount them properly. I could make a start right away.'

She gathered the photos up carefully and tucked them back into a folder.

'I'll walk across with you,' Richard said, 'I want something from the office.'

On their way over, Jane raised a hand to wave to Gareth, working on the trellising on the top garden.

'I know I said I wouldn't interfere or give you advice . . . ' Richard began.

'But you're going to anyway.'

'It looks like it.'

Jane stopped, one foot on the low wall. 'Out with it, then, though I can't imagine it's anything I haven't thought of for myself already.'

'All right. But I do still feel responsible for you, you know. After all, I did drag you up here.'

'Yes, screaming. Now what is it?'

Richard glanced in Gareth's direction and then looked back at his daughter. 'When Martin arrived, something inside me said you were probably going to get on. Well, more than that, to be honest. More than just getting on, I mean. He's good-looking and intelligent, you seem to have things in common. I could see that he was struck by you the very first time he saw you.'

'Go on.'

'But Gareth now. I mean, there's nothing wrong with him. Far from it. He's different from Martin in almost every way and I can see the attraction, but . . . '

'Out with it.'

'Okay. At the end of this year, you're going back to college and Gareth will be staying here. You'll meet a lot of people, more like Martin than Gareth ever will be.'

'So what's the point of all this?'

'Jane, do I have to spell it out?'

'Yes.'

'I don't want to see you getting hurt. Or Gareth, for that matter. If you spend too much time with him, if you get too involved . . . '

'Don't worry.'

'If you get too involved, then leaving is going to be awful.'

'I said, don't worry.'

'As long as you're clear that whatever happens it's got to end at the end of the year. It's got to end next summer.'

'I know that. Gareth knows that. Whatever happens between us, whatever happens here, I know it isn't going to be forever. Dad, I don't want a relationship that's going to last forever. I'm eighteen; I'm too young for that.' She touched his arm. 'I'm not in a hurry to get myself sorted out and settled down. Maybe at the back of my mind I do think that it is possible that one day I'll fall in love and it will be for ever — but that isn't going to happen yet.'

'You really think you can control these things?'

'I think that knowing what you want helps.'

'Sure,' said Richard, not sounding all that sure at all. By the time he had known for certain what he wanted, it had been too late.

'What I want – the most important thing for me – is college and professional know-how. I'm going to get myself established in what I want to do. That's the rest of my life: how I'll earn my living; express myself; show what I feel about things.'

'What about people, Jane? Won't you need to show how you feel about them?'

Jane linked her arm with his and started to walk with him down towards the centre. As they passed, budding poets lurked in the shrubbery, composing haiku.

'It's not going to be all enlargers and developing fluids, Dad. At least, I hope not. But remember I'm only eighteen.' She squeezed his arm and laughed. 'I'll probably fall in love half-a-dozen times before I'm twenty.'

She stopped abruptly and swung round to face him.

'That's going to hurt a lot. Breaking up. It's like, I don't know . . . '

'Like dying?' Richard suggested.

'Yes, like dying. Only you know you'll wake up one morning and you'll be alive again. Especially . . . ' she gave him a quick glance of sympathy, ' . . . when you're young.'

'You mean young hearts mend fast.'

'Something like that.'

'And if you make mistakes, you've got time to get over them.'

Jane heard the sorrow in his voice, saw it in his eyes. She knew there was nothing she could do to ease that away. Only time would achieve that: and even then a small residue of the pain would linger, somewhere at the bottom of his heart, like a smooth hard stone.

She knew that one day it might be like that for her, too. One day when the ache was bad enough to stick and when all you saw on that spring morning when life was spreading out all around you was your own chance of happiness faintly fading into the distance.

'Jane!'

She turned at the sound of a voice from one of the upstairs windows.

'I've been looking for you.'

Martin was hanging out and smiling down, a sheaf of papers in his hand.

'I'll run along,' said Richard, touching Jane lightly on the shoulder and then raising a hand towards Martin in greeting.

'You won't find me up there,' Jane called.

'Hang on! I'll be down.'

'I've got things to do,' she shouted after him, but he was already on his way.

She went and stood at the edge of the garden, leaning forward on the iron railings which separated the garden from the sloping field careering down to the river below. A few cattle wandered aimlessly about, while others stood like oversize toy models for a game of farms. There was still a haze over the far end of the valley, shielding the tops of the trees and pierced only by the three mill chimneys. She shivered involuntarily, recalling her misery of that night. So short a time ago and then she had felt everything collapsing about her – her father, herself, the year here on these wonderful moors. But already that seemed in so many ways like a dream, something that had happened to somebody else, not to her. It was like a photograph she had watched taking shape but which had been left too long: the outlines had darkened, thickened out, disappeared into memory.

'Here you are!'

'What's so important?'

Martin waved the sheets of paper in her face. 'These.'

Jane shook her folder at him. 'And these.'

'Poems,' said Martin.

'Photographs,' said Jane.

He rested one foot on the low wall, close against the railings. Those blue eyes of his! The fingers that tapped against his poems were long and their skin seemed soft, unlike Gareth's, hard and calloused from hours spent in the gardens. For a second Jane imagined Martin's fingers touching her, smooth against her face.

'I'll show you mine, if you'll show me yours,' Martin laughed.

'I bet you say that to all the girls.'

'Not since I was six – or was it seven?'

'What happened?'

'Nancy Spurling hit me across the knuckles with her ruler and I ran home crying.'

'Serves you right!'

'I expect so.'

He leaned back against the railings and looked up at the sky. 'It's a beautiful day for a walk.'

Something turned slowly inside Jane's stomach; a few tiny waves of warning spread through her veins. Away past the house, out of sight but clear in her mind, she knew Gareth was labouring away: she knew that later he would come to find her and they would walk up on to the tops together.

She gave Martin a smile. 'Some other time.'

'Oh, come on!'

Jane moved away, folder held in front of her as if somehow it was going to ward him off – sort of garlic against Dracula. Only none of the films she'd seen had given Dracula eyes like the ones staring at her now, doing their practised best to get her to change her mind.

'No, I mean it.' She looked meaningfully at the folder. 'Work.'

'Then at least let me see them.'

'Later.'

'I'd like to show you what I've written, now it's less dreadful. He started to walk towards her as Jane retreated. 'I'd like to know what you think. Honestly.'

'Honestly?' echoed Jane mockingly.

'Why do you think I was looking for you?'

She laughed: 'I can't imagine.'

Martin followed her between the pecking hens and the piles of logs waiting for the winter; they rounded the house and began to move towards the barn.

'You're determined, aren't you?'

'Of course.'

He gave an exaggerated sigh of acceptance. 'Very well. But do me one favour.' He held the poems out towards her. 'Take these with you. Have a look at them when you get a minute. Fifteen seconds even. However long it takes between exposures.'

'Even I can't read in the dark,' Jane replied playfully. But she did take the sheets of paper and slid them down into her folder before she turned away.

'You'll have to let me know what you think,' Martin said, calling after her.

The door opened and closed without answer. Martin stood there for a moment or two and then went back into the house.

What both of them had been fully conscious of all through this last part of their conversation, though neither of them had mentioned it, was Gareth, up on the top garden, looking at and listening to everything that took place.

Chapter 15

Jane zipped her anorak tight and rewound her scarf about her neck. The sun was a watery orange filtering through a drift of cloud and a north-east wind skimmed the heather. She began to have some sense of what it would be like in the winter, when drifts of snow would block the track between house and village and they would huddle round roaring log fires and try to forget about the patterns of ice forming on the windows.

As she looked down at the mottled earth, bits and pieces of Martin's poems slipped across her mind.

coarse grass grasps the skyline
harsh against the fall of sun

echoes of light on veins of chalk
red bricks melt into grass

She walked and the phrases folded against one another, at one and the same time separate, yet parts of a single poem that was Martin: his feelings, his way of looking at the world. For Jane it was a collection of photographs, moments taken out of time and made different because he had seen them differently.

Like her pictures.

And one especially: not typed like the rest but written in small, slanting lines across the back of the last page, maybe not a whole poem at all.

> *I thought I had left you behind*
> *But find in others' eyes*
> *The brightness of your own*
> *The softness of your skin*
> *On every stone.*

Something direct and personal brought Jane close, she felt, to Martin's feelings, whereas the other writing had held her back, kept her at a distance. Bending, she picked a fragment of stone from the ground and held it in the palm of her hand, wondering who Martin had written that poem for. She thought about her father and Karen: of the future for Gareth and herself.

She closed her eyes and gripped the piece of stone as hard as she could and when she looked again the landscape had changed. As far as she could see it was freckled with white; about her a light snow was falling soundlessly, soft upon her face.

> *The softness of your skin*
> *On every stone*

Gareth stood in the distance, the dark curls round his face fringed with white. She tried to bring him closer, wanting to read the expression on his face but she could not. Each second, he slipped further and further back until he was no more than a dark speck on the horizon. Then not even that.

The snow began to fall harder.

She was cold.

Only the stone in her hand seemed real.

Jane looked up at the sky and then, again, closed her eyes.

'Hey!'

The sudden voice broke the silence, brought her daydream to an end. Turning, she saw Gareth hurrying across the moor towards her: a moor empty of snow.

'What on earth were you up to?'

'What d'you mean?'

'Standing there like that. Gazing off into space as if you were in some kind of trance.'

'Oh, I don't know. Perhaps I was.'

She grinned at him reassuringly and tried to clear the doubt from his brown, watchful eyes.

'Why didn't you wait for me?'

'I left a note.'

'I know. That's why I'm here.'

'Let's go then.'

She took his hand and at the same moment dropped the piece of stone behind her back.

'How long have you got?'

'Oh, an hour or so. How about you?'

'About the same.' She looked at him, seeing that something was still troubling him but not wanting to ask exactly what. 'Let's not waste it.'

They began to walk briskly across the moor.

Jane could tell from Gareth's manner that something

was wrong; it was partly the way he walked, partly the hasty answers to her questions about where they were going, the things they saw. He was almost abrupt, as if the words had to be forced out. At the back of it all, she knew, there was something that to him was more important and she wondered how long she would have to wait to know (although she could guess) exactly what it was.

They were turning for home when it came.

'You going to tell me then?'

'What?'

'Going to let me in on it?'

'Gareth, let you in on what?'

'What you were thinking about back there, gawping off into space?'

'I wasn't gawping.'

'I don't know what else you'd call it.'

'Well, I do.'

They trudged another couple of hundred yards; for both of them any sense of pleasure had gone out of the walk. It was simply something they had to do, nothing more or less. Jane's feet stumbled against a tuft of coarse grass and Gareth whirled his head as if to say, what else can you expect?

At the wall, he asked again.

'Are you or aren't you?'

(Oh, God! thought Jane.)

'Aren't I what?' she said.

'Telling me.'

She sighed and walked in a small circle, shaking her

head. When she did look at him again, he was glaring at her, anger visible in the concentration on his face and the tenseness of his body.

'I was thinking about a poem.'

'Which poem?'

'You wouldn't know it,' she answered, the words out of her mouth before she realized how hurtful they might seem.

'Oh, right!' His boot kicked hard against the base of the stone. 'Of course, if it's a poem, then Gareth wouldn't know it from a hole in the ground. Best stick to what he knows: roses and cabbages and stuff like that.'

'Gareth, that wasn't what I meant.'

'Wasn't it?'

'No, and you know it.'

'That's as maybe.'

He hunched his shoulders and jammed his hands deep into his pockets. In one heavy movement he was over the wall and striding down the hillside towards the centre. Jane hesitated for a few moments before scrambling after him.

'Whose poem?' was all he said when she came alongside.

'Martin's.'

'I knew it!'

'Then why ask?'

'Because . . . ' His hand was tight about her wrist; his eyes were on fire as his head jutted towards her. ' . . . I wanted to hear you say it. Admit it.'

'You make it sound as if it's a crime.'

'Waste of time, more like. Mooning around over some rubbish . . .'

'It wasn't rubbish! And I wasn't mooning around!'

'That's what you say.'

'Yes, it is.' She shook her arm, trying to break his grip. 'Now let me go!'

He didn't seem to hear her. His grip tightened until Jane could feel the strength of his fingers biting into the bone. Her skin was twisted and burning.

'Let me . . .'

'Love poem, was it?' Gareth asked scornfully.

'What difference . . . ?'

'Was it?' he shouted in her face.

'Yes.'

Gareth pushed her away from him and she stumbled backwards, falling awkwardly to the ground.

'I knew it,' he said. 'I knew it!'

'But it wasn't for me,' Jane cried. 'It wasn't written for me.'

If Gareth heard her or not, she couldn't tell. He was on his way towards the house, cutting diagonally across the grass and bracken, half-running, eager to be rid of her.

Jane took her time getting up, not wanting to rush after Gareth, trying to understand his frustration and the causes of his behaviour. If he saw things the way her father did — Martin being 'right' for her, whatever that might mean, and himself being wrong — then his jealousy was easy to appreciate, even though that didn't mean she approved of the way he had acted. And in a sense that she thought she could understand a little, if Gareth imagined she had been lost in the feelings that had come from one of Martin's poems up there on *his*, Gareth's beloved moors, then that jealousy would be all the stronger.

What depths had Heathcliff's jealousy driven him to?

What had been his feeling when Cathy had chosen to marry another man instead of himself?

You loved me – then what right had you to leave me? . . . I have not broken your heart – you have broken it – and in breaking it, you have broken mine. So much the worse for me, that I am strong. Do I want to live? What kind of living will it be when you – oh, God! would you like to live with your soul in the grave?

And much of Heathcliff's fiery jealousy came from the fact that he was certain he had been cast aside because of his roughness, his lack of class and good breeding; he had been passed over for a more sensitive, better educated man.

When Jane reached the centre, her father was waiting for her in the yard, white-faced. She knew instinctively that whatever was wrong was something to do with Gareth.

'Tell me,' she said.

'Gareth came storming back in here just as Martin was coming out of the house. He ran right at him and knocked him down. I had to get help to pull him off.'

Jane's hands went to her face; she didn't know what to do, what to say.

'Martin's lying down. He'll be all right, I think, but I've sent for the doctor, just as a precaution.'

'And Gareth?'

Richard looked at her, surprised at her apparent concern.

'I told him to get off the premises and not to come back.'

Jane clenched and unclenched her fists. Anything she said then would come out wrong, she knew that. She ran into the house, not wanting her father to see the tears that were welling up in her eyes.

Chapter 16

Martin was lying in the attic bed, propped up against three pillows: personal stereo in place; notebook open on the covers, green pen between his fingers. A length of sticking plaster was fastened across his right eye, angled from the bridge of his nose to the far end of his eyebrow. His left cheek was grazed and a small cut bisected the swelling at the corner of his mouth.

As Jane put her head round the door, he dropped the pen on to the bed and grinned.

'You don't give up, do you?' she said, coming into the room.

'No point in wasting good real-life experience. I've never been knocked down in a jealous fury before.'

'Is that what it was?'

Martin grinned winningly. 'He wasn't objecting to the colour of my shirts – although Gareth probably doesn't approve of those, either.'

Jane stood close to the head of the bed, looking down. 'Are you okay? I mean, really.'

'The doctor says if I'm lucky I've got two or three days.'

'To live?'

Martin laughed. 'To stay in bed.'

'No broken bones, then?'

He shook his head and then winced at the sharpness of the movement. 'A couple of badly bruised ribs, some bruising around the kidney area – what you can see –' he gestured towards his face '– but that apart . . . Besides, you should see the other feller.'

'Gareth? Is he badly hurt too?'

'Not a scratch.'

Jane paused for a moment and then joined in Martin's laughter. Relaxed, she sat on the edge of the bed. Martin looked at her seriously and then took her hand.

'He must think an awful lot of you to react like that.'

'If it was because of me.'

'Wasn't it?'

Jane nodded, tight-lipped.

'Did he think we were . . . ?' Martin left the sentence unfinished: his look was enough to make the meaning clear.

'It was those poems you showed me.'

'God! I've had bad critical reactions to what I write before now, but no one's ever beaten me up!'

'I don't mean that.'

'You'd better explain.'

'When Gareth found me on the top, I was thinking about one of your poems. Saying it over in my mind. That was what made him jealous. I think partly because it made him feel inferior . . . '

'That's ridiculous!'

'I know that. But it's not difficult to see why he might think that way.'

'And what's the other part of the reason?'

It took Jane a while to answer, to get the words right in her head. 'When I first arrived, I think Gareth was – I don't know – scared of me in some way. He use to watch me, follow me sometimes, I think. As though he wanted to talk to me but didn't dare. It's partly some stupid idea he's got about being less intelligent than the people who come here: artists, writers, people like that. Like you. And also because he works for Dad and, in a kind of a way, for me too. Even when we've spent some time together it hasn't been around the Centre: here he gets on with his work and I get on with mine. The only times Gareth feels he can be close to me is when we're up on the moors, which he feels are his territory.

'So, seeing me up there thinking about you, about something you'd written – that started it all off. If I'd reacted differently at the time, maybe I could have made him see, but I didn't and he came charging down here and . . .'

'Ran smack into me,' Martin finished for her.

'I'm afraid so.'

'It's okay. Most great writers spent half their lives in their sick beds. Those that didn't die before they were twenty. I've just about avoided that.'

'I'm glad.'

Jane looked down at the bed, where Martin's hand still held hers. Slowly he withdrew it and began to toy with his pen.

'So if I had been about to show an interest, a personal interest, I mean . . .'

Jane smiled wryly. 'I should have been flattered but said thank you but I was already interested, as you put it, in somebody else.'

'Gareth?'

'Gareth.'

Martin leant back against the pillows; in truth, he didn't seem too displeased.

'What about the girl?' Jane asked.

'Which girl is this exactly?'

'Exactly the girl you thought you had left behind.'

'But found in others' eyes?'

'That's the one.'

Martin shook his head again, winced again. 'I suppose I'm getting over her. Slowly.'

'Is that why you came here?'

'Sort of, I guess. The place came up at an appropriate time. Yorkshire's far enough from Scotland for the distance to mean something. Eventually.'

'I'm sorry,' Jane said, meaning it not just for Martin, but also for her father, for Gareth . . . and for herself. At the end of the year the distance she would be putting between Nottingham and Yorkshire, between herself and Gareth would be just as important, just as difficult.

She stood up and went to the door.

'Can I fetch you anything?'

'How about a cup of tea?'

'Okay.'

'Then when you come back there's a proposition I want to make to you.'

'I thought we'd just been through that,' Jane laughed.

'This one's different.'

'That's what they all say.'

It was Martin's turn to laugh. Painfully. 'I've started writing some stuff about the landscape, the moors, those old mill chimneys, and I wondered if you'd be interested in doing a book. Together. Your photographs and my poems. I know a printer who . . . '

Before he could finish Jane had pushed him back and was kissing him quickly but enthusiastically on the side of the face, narrowly missing his cuts and bruises. When she pulled her face clear it was creased with smiles.

'Do I take it that means you're interested?' said Martin, recovering.

'You bet I am! Now just wait while I get some tea

and I'll bring up those pictures I was enlarging. I think there are some there that might be just what you're looking for.'

And she bounced out of the room, taking the stairs two at a time down to the foot of the house, singing at the top of her voice as she went.

Her father stood near the archway between the house and their cottage, staring out over the valley. The cattle in the field had gathered close together around the trough, tails unmethodically swishing away flies that hummed blue in the afternoon sunlight.

'I'm sorry,' Jane said softly, almost startling him.

'Whatever for?' Richard turned to face her, worry lines etched into his face.

'All that business earlier.'

'I don't see that it's your fault.'

'I'm afraid it is. Most of it, anyway.'

'Gareth just can't control his temper, that's all there is to it.'

(Neither could Heathcliff, Jane thought.)

'If we hadn't dragged him away from Martin when we did,' Richard went on, 'heaven only knows what damage might have been done.'

Jane picked a flake of black paint away from the railings and watched as it spiralled lazily away from her fingers, down and down towards the trodden grass of the field.

'If I'd talked to him up on the top instead of reacting

the way I did, it need never have happened. I mean, it one thing for me to understand the kind of relationship I want with Gareth, it's quite another for him to understand what's going on inside my head. I've got to talk to him – about us and about Martin and myself. Then he can make his own choices; he can carry on seeing me or not. But, Dad, you can't sack him for what happened today.'

'I already have.'

'Then tell him you were too hasty. Tell him you've changed your mind.'

'What if I haven't?'

'Come on, Dad! You're jumping off at half-cock and punishing him for jumping off at half-cock in the first place.'

'I'm stopping our residents from getting beaten up, that's what I'm doing.'

'That won't get the gardening done.'

'Jane, there are plenty of other gardeners.'

'But only one Gareth.'

Richard lifted his head and looked skywards; he turned and leaned against the railing, struggling to come to the right decision, trying to reconcile his duty with his feelings for Jane – trying to understand her feelings for Gareth.

'Listen, Dad, I told you the other day; I'm not going to get myself tied down. I'm not looking for a relationship that's meant to last for ever. But I'm here for a year, just one year. Gareth's here too. There's no get-

that. If you fire him that won't drive him
. He'll always be here – or somewhere up there –
up on his precious moor.'

She looked up beyond the wall of the upper garden
to the edge of the tops. The rough stone was outlined
against the sky, the sun beginning to slide down to
meet it. There was no one in sight: the moor was bare.

'So what do you want to do? What do you want me
to do?'

Jane looked back at him and gave a half-smile. 'I
want you to talk to him. Read him the riot act by all
means. Suggest he goes to Martin and says he's sorry.
Whatever. As for what I'm going to do—' she traced a
criss-cross pattern in the dirt with the toe of her shoe
'—I'm going to be as open with him as I can. Explain
how I feel; that I want to spend as much time with him
while I'm here as I can, as much time as doing all the
other things I want to do will allow. But that at the end
of the year it's going to be over. He's got to know that.'

'You make it sound so easy.'

Jane shook her head, aware that he was thinking
about himself and the woman whose love he had lost –
both the women whose love he had lost.

'I know it isn't easy. I think I'm old enough to
understand there's no easy way of saying goodbye.
Somebody's always going to be hurt. I do know that. I
just think it's got to be easier if you're aware before-
hand that it's going to happen.'

Richard took her hands in his. 'You sound tough
and sensible and I hope it works. For both your sakes.'

124

'So do I, Dad. So do I.'

She lifted her head and kissed him and as she pulled away something made her turn. The sun had dipped to the level of the wall and was beginning to filter orange light along the horizon. As she watched, a figure appeared just beyond the wall, dark-haired, tall, striding out towards the heights. Jane gave her father a quick smile and hurried away, leaving Richard to watch as she climbed the hill, hopes for her happiness clenched as tight and sure as stones caught in the hand.

Pam Lyons
Odd Girl Out £1.25

When sixteen-year-old Claire loses both her parents in a tragic car accident, she finds herself uprooted from her home and sent to live with her wealthy aunt and uncle down south.

Driving herself hard – and keeping sympathetic friends at arms' length – Claire allows herself time off from her studies only for her one passion – sport. But the high wall that she had built around her emotions slowly begins to crumble when Claire is selected as the School's youngest-ever netball captain – and tall, attractive Geoff Binyon ambles up to congratulate her – and to tell her she is someone 'special'!

Danny's Girl 85p

For sixteen-year-old Wendy, life was pretty straight forward. She enjoyed her tomboy existence with her parents and brother Mike on their farm in Norfolk. Then, late one sunny September afternoon, Danny wandered into her life and suddenly Wendy's happy and uncomplicated world is turned upside-down. Unsure of how she should behave or what is expected of her, she allows herself to be carried along in Danny's wake, and when he finds himself in trouble at his exclusive boarding school she is his only ally. Eventually, Wendy's fierce loyalty to the boy she loves leads them both deeper and deeper into trouble . . .

Latchkey Girl 85p

Ronnie was an only child and, compared with her young, glamorous parents with their interesting lives, pretty much of an 'ugly duckling' too. Only Gran, it seems, really loves her. But, when Gran's illness means she must come and live with her son and his family, Ronnie's problems come to a head and she is forced into a bold choice . . .

David S. Williams
Give Me Back My Pride £1.25

Her mother's illness cut across Dianne's happy life like a knife.
Suddenly the double demands of home and school became almost
too much to bear. There seems no one with whom she can share her
problems, not even her boyfriend, David. Then she meets Jago, the
outcast – the guy with the bad reputation whom nobody
understands. For a time she shares his reckless life – until she has to
choose between Jago and loyalty to herself.

Forgive and Forget £1.25

Claire's life was in turmoil when her family moved to Wales. It meant
leaving Simon, the guy who meant so much to her, and she was
determined *never* to like her new home. But the rugged beauty of the
countryside and the compelling friendliness of the people soothed
away her resentment. And then she met Gareth, a dark-eyed Welsh
boy who captivated her with his infectious grin . . .

All these books are available at your local bookshop or newsagent,
or can be ordered direct from the publisher. Indicate the number of
copies required and fill in the form below

....

Name ————————————————————————————————————
(Block letters please)

Address ————————————————————————————————————

————————————————————————————————————

Send to CS Department, Pan Books Ltd
PO Box 40, Basingstoke, Hants
Please enclose remittance to the value of the cover price plus:
35p for the first book plus 15p per copy for each additional book
ordered to a maximum charge of £1.25 to cover postage and
packing
Applicable only in the UK

While every effort is made to keep prices low, it is sometimes
necessary to increase prices at short notice. Pan Books reserve the
right to show on covers and charge new retail prices which may
differ from those advertised in the text or elsewhere